Alaina Marie

JOHN HENRY BRANCH

authorHOUSE®

AuthorHouse™
1663 Liberty Drive
Bloomington, IN 47403
www.authorhouse.com
Phone: 833-262-8899

Published by AuthorHouse 04/22/2021

ISBN: 978-1-6655-2272-4 (sc)
ISBN: 978-1-6655-2270-0 (hc)
ISBN: 978-1-6655-2271-7 (e)

Library of Congress Control Number: 2021907587

Print information available on the last page.

Contents

So many of my friends and family have played a part in making the publication of this sequel to *Concho* come to fruition. I would never have even attempted it were it not for the encouragement of so many who read *Concho* and pressed me to continue the story. To name them all would be impossible. However, I do want to dedicate this work to those who assisted in its completion. First of all, my loving wife, Cathy, who inspired me to tackle the first book, my family members who read the rough draft and nudged me to continue the process of publication (you know who you are), my attorney friend, David Thiel, who gave me guidance concerning legal procedure and protocol. I dedicate it to my granddaughter, Kassidy Jae Branch, for her labor of love and her magnificent artistry in producing the cover design. I dedicate it to friends and family members whose names are used as characters in the story. I do this in honor of their friendship that has made my life so pleasurable. Finally, and most importantly, I dedicate this work to my niece, Sherry Marie Carter Whitten. No, it is no accident that her middle name appears in the title of the book. She, along with my sister, Marie Hill, are responsible for my selection of the name, Alaina Marie. Sherry contributed a great deal of time helping me with portions of the story as well as final editing and preparation for publication. My greatest gratitude to one and all.

Being involved in pioneer missions for the Southern Baptist Convention in Wyoming, I was often presented with the opportunity to travel back and forth across the state. The fact that I was bi-vocational while pastoring small mission churches provided many different experiences in the outdoors. I worked at whatever was available to provide for my family. I drove school buses, worked on ranches and on farms, cut timber for lumber, etc., etc. All of that, coupled with my love for the outdoors, took me into the back country and wilderness areas all across the state—from the Grand Tetons, Yellowstone Park and the Yellowstone River in the north, to the Snowy Range, The Grand Encampment, and the Platte River in the south, from the Devil's Tower in the east, to the Flaming Gorge in the west.

I worked alongside native Wyoming residents and heard their stories about the pioneer days in the Wyoming territory, how their parents and grandparents came there for a fresh start and carved a life from the harsh, Wyoming terrain. I often made it a point to travel the back roads and trails, exploring places where a human foot rarely fell. I rode and packed horseback along the Continental Divide, from the old ghost town of Battle, southward to the Wyoming/Colorado state line.

In all of these different roles, I experienced both the harshness and the beauty of that semi-arid climate. A white-out blizzard with temperatures forty below zero and winds of fifty miles per hour can still claim the life of someone caught unprepared out on the roadways. On the other hand, springtime brings the lush, nutritious, green grass that carpets the foothills like a well-manicured lawn as far as the eye can see. I have visited the old pioneer trails where the hundreds of wagon wheels cut into the rocks and banks leave a testimony of the grit and determination that fueled the pioneer movement westward to the shores of the Pacific Ocean.

As I witnessed these things, I often considered the hardships, pain and suffering both physical and emotional, that were endured by those who dared to take on such a challenge. I believe that those years I spent in wild, wonderful Wyoming and the pioneer spirit I witnessed there, inspired a new determination within myself...a determination to enjoy the wonderful life God has blessed me with and to meet, head on, any hardship or challenge that life might bring and consider it a part of the ride that will soon be conquered, no matter what the cost. The number of days of this life is not certain but eternity hereafter is. So, I will enjoy the beauty of God's creation here while I can but try never to take my eyes off of the horizon that leads into the hereafter.

Somewhere along the way, during those years in Wyoming, a story began to form in my mind. It was a story about a man and his dream to develop a strain of horses that would be perfect to meet the many demands of the American frontier, the hardships that befell his family, and how those difficulties were met and the dream realized. It was a story that became *Concho*. The story wasn't complete, however. A man's children become his heart and soul. His young daughter echoed his adventurous spirit and the desire to protect the helpless and right the wrong. In the end, the entire family embarks on a wild adventure as they put everything on the line to uphold law and order and prevent a terrible injustice to an entire town. Leading the way for the cause of justice on her spirited grulla stallion is young *Alaina Marie*.

A story about a girl and a horse on the western frontier.

1. The Long Journey

The westbound train lumbered along through the foothills of the Shoshone Mountain Range of Central Nevada as though it had no particular place to be. The afternoon sun, magnified by the window glasses, had warmed the inside of the Pullman railcar—and made Alaina almost forget the autumn chill of the early morning.

The magnificent coach was one of the finest available to any rail service. It boasted of being constructed by the Pullman Palace Car Company and featured plush carpeting, draperies, a library, and even card tables, as well as sleeping births that were attached above the upholstered chairs. The company trademark phrase was, *'Travel and Sleep in Safety and Comfort.'* However, after several days of travel and sleep, the novelty of it all had fairly worn off.

Alaina had passed the long day rehashing the events that had prompted her to even dream of making a journey to California. It had begun with her mother, Emma Catherine (Calhoun) Johnson, taking on a client for a court case in San Francisco. The client was an old friend of the family and trusted no one but Catherine Johnson, the first woman in the state of Wyoming to become an attorney, to represent him. Of course, the success Cat Johnson had acquired over the years of winning her court cases probably played a part in his interest in retaining her services, as well.

Whatever the reason, her mother had agreed to represent him under the impression that it could be settled in a matter of a few weeks, a month at the most. Complications had arisen, however, and three months had passed without much progress. There were piles of documents and records

1

that needed to be reviewed and sorted through. Catherine had neither the time to do it herself, nor did she know of anyone that she trusted to do it for her. So, reluctantly, she had wired Alaina, asking if she would be willing to come to San Francisco and be her assistant throughout the trial.

Alaina still wasn't sure why she had decided to come. Sitting at a desk inside a dark, drab room sorting through boring receipts and papers was the farthest thing from something enjoyable to her. She had spent every minute of her life since she was old enough to climb into a saddle outdoors with the cows and horses and hired ranch hands on her father's ranch. She was familiar with every hill, valley, stream and mountain between Cheyenne, Rawlins and Casper, and most of the country even further north and west towards Lander.

Her hair was bleached, and her skin was tanned by the Wyoming sun. About the time she'd learned to walk, her father, Tall Johnson, began teaching her pretty much everything he knew about the outdoors. With his skillful instruction, riding, roping, shooting and even handling a bow and arrow had become second nature to her. He had seemed content with her as his daily companion while her brother, Jesse, poured over books about law and politics. It seemed inevitable from the beginning that Jesse would follow in his mother's footsteps while Alaina followed in her dad's.

Jesse would be the one to be of greater assistance to his mom in San Francisco, but he was attending college back east, all the way up in New Haven, Connecticut. He had set his mind to be the best attorney in the country and had sought out the best learning institution on the continent. Alaina's family was not wealthy, but they were far from poor, and both of her parents had agreed to make any sacrifices necessary to assure their children had a proper education for whatever profession they chose. Jesse had chosen to study law at Yale University.

Alaina, on the other hand, was content with her ability to read, write and cipher numbers. She could count the number of livestock in a herd more quickly and accurately than any of the other hands on the ranch. She could add, subtract and divide with a correct figure every time, and as far as she was concerned, that was all of the book learning she needed. Nevertheless, her mother had insisted she become familiar with the classics in literature, including poetry and prose, and she demanded that Alaina acquire proper usage of the King's English. To Alaina's way of thinking, the things she learned from her father about survival in the outdoors was much more useful than all of the formal schooling in the world.

The work on the ranch had slowed with the coming of fall, however, and the mountains would soon be covered with a deep blanket of snow, hindering her wanderings and adventures for the time being. San Francisco was somewhat of an alluring city from what she had read, and besides, if her mother wanted and needed her help, Alaina felt she would be a very poor and unappreciative daughter to deny her request.

By now, the trip had gone from boring to almost unbearable. She felt as if she had practically grown to the seat of the Pullman. The only opportunity for any meaningful break was when they stopped to take on water for the steam engine. During those stops, she had enough time to check on her horse, Badger, whom she had refused to leave behind. Sometimes she even had enough time to take him from the boxcar for some exercise.

The past two days hadn't offered many of those opportunities, though. The stations were stretched farther and farther apart as they traveled through the desert regions of Utah and Nevada, sometimes pushing their water supply to its limit. Entering the mountains once again had provided a bit of entertainment for a while with all of the beautiful colors of autumn foliage. However, in her opinion, the Shoshone Range of Central Nevada couldn't compare to the Laramie's of Wyoming. They soon became repetitious and mundane to the point that she finally rolled her sheepskin coat into a pillow and leaned against the window, allowing herself to doze periodically as the car rocked back and forth along the track.

* * *

Alaina snapped upright and looked around the car in bewilderment as she felt the train begin to lurch and brake to a stop. Looking through the window opposite her, she realized that they had been climbing higher into the Humboldt Mountain Range for quite some time. They had crested over a mountain pass and had barely just begun to descend the other side when the engineer brought them to an abrupt halt. She noticed that the road base for the tracks hugged the mountain on her side of the car but dropped sharply downward on the other side, blending into the steep decent of the mountain slope to a valley far below.

She was about to make her way to the front of the car to inquire as to why they had stopped in such an implausible location when the conductor came down the aisle explaining that the mountain had caved off onto the tracks and they would be there for a while. Passengers were permitted to leave the car, so Alaina's thoughts immediately focused on her best friend and trusted mount, Badger, who was accompanying her on the trip. She carefully picked her way, stepping on the ends of the railroad ties back to the boxcar to check on him. She gave him a handful of grain from her saddlebag and then bent some hay straw together to form a makeshift brush and gave him a quick rubdown.

Her father had taught her how to do that, among other things. He was adamant about giving the best care possible to your mount. He always said that if you took care of your horse, when the going got rough your horse would take care of you. Badger had been her special birthday gift from her father on her sixteenth birthday. Of course, Badger wasn't just any ole ordinary horse. He was, in fact, one of the best foals from her father's breeding program. He was sired by her father's pride and joy, Concho, and foaled by one of his best mares.

Badger was what her father called a grulla color, pronounced grew-ya. He was sort of between buckskin and blue roan, actually more of a mouse color. His mane and tail were black. A dark, almost black dorsal stripe ran the length of his back, and stripes of that same color began at his withers, ran down his shoulders, and reached almost to his girth. His legs were darker from the knees down, with dark colored bars wrapping around them from his elbow to his knees. Books she had read indicated that those markings were a throwback to the early pre-historic equine species.

There were very few like him. Not just because of the color, but more so because of his disposition and character, as well as his confirmation. Her father had wrestled with whether giving her a stallion was a good idea, but having watched her breaking and training horses since she was just a child, he was convinced she could hold her own with any four-legged beast with as much savvy and grit as any man he knew.

Alaina had proven him to be correct in his assessment. For the past year and a half, she and Badger had become the best of friends. They seemed to have a connection seldom seen between man and animal. When she decided to come on this trip, the first arrangement she made was to assure Badger would be making it with her. To leave him in the care of the ranch hands for God knew how long, was something she wasn't prepared to do. Besides, she hated the thought of being in a strange place with no transportation. That would be the nearest thing to prison she could imagine.

Alaina was about to climb down from the boxcar when she noticed the conductor and three other men making their way toward her. One of the men she supposed to be the engineer because of his railroad attire, but the other two were dressed in a fashion more familiar to her world. One wore a brown suit with shiny, dark brown boots. The strings of his black bowtie flapped in the strong breeze against his crisp, white shirt. He reminded Alaina of some prominent rancher who knew his worth.

The man walking with an important air beside him was probably the man's foreman. His black felt hat was dusty and stained. His wild rag, or bandana, was stained and dirty, suggesting too many weeks without soap and water. He wore black leather boots that were quite lackluster and worn, fringe-edged chaps, and spurs that seemed to Alaina to produce a little too much jingle as he walked. Closer inspection confirmed her suspicion. The cowboy had jingle bobs attached to the rowels. Each one consisted of a star, a bell and a cross.

Alaina caught herself scoffing under her breath and thinking that no self-respecting cowboy, or cowgirl for that matter, ought to be caught dead with such nonfunctional trinkets attached to their gear. She knew of their original purpose and that in some parts they actually had a place. Cowboys and vaqueros from Texas and Mexico believed the jingling noise would set an inconspicuous diamondback to rattling, therefore issuing a warning as to his whereabouts.

True, there were rattlers in some parts of the mountainous states, and she had occasionally crossed paths with them on her father's ranch. After all, the mountain range that stretched through that area of Wyoming was called "The Rattlesnakes" for a reason, but the small species there hardly provided enough danger to a cowboy to warrant wearing such showy paraphernalia as jingle bobs on your spurs. Most prairie rattlers and sidewinders she had seen weren't large enough to be of danger to anyone wearing high-topped boots, and they were normally more concerned with getting out of your way than trying to bite you.

She had only heard of one occasion when a cowboy was bitten and that was because of his own drunken display of tomfoolery. He had convinced himself and the other boys in camp that he could hypnotize the snake by looking into its eyes. As he held the viper near his face, it drew back as if in submissive regress so he moved in closer only to have the rattler launch forward to sink its fangs in the soft flesh right between the cowboy's eyes.

He survived the bite, however. The doctor reckoned it was by one of two possibilities. One, the cowboy had previously been attempting to milk the snake's venom into a tin cup in order to see exactly what poison looked like and probably depleted the venom sacs. Or two, because he had practically polished off an entire bottle of cheap whiskey since sundown that day. Alaina knew the first possibility was more accurate because of the effect alcohol had on a body's blood. It would more than likely make the poison more effective.

The four men had been carefully choosing their steps along the slippery roadbed toward her. When they reached the boxcar, the conductor asked politely, "Miss, is this your horse?"

"Yes," she replied. "Why do you want to know?"

"Well, we're in a fix here," he explained. He motioned vaguely over his shoulder with a thumb pointing toward the disaster. "That rockslide is way too big for us to remove. In fact, it will take a whole crew at least a week to make this track passable." He nodded toward 'ole jingle bob' who was eyeing Badger up and down as if trying to decide if he was worth his salt. "We need to borrow your horse for Jackson here to go on to the next rail station and let them know about this blockage. Meantime, we will have to back down the mountain to wait until they can come clear the track."

"No one is borrowing my horse, mister," Alaina bristled instantly, not liking the way the cowhand was looking Badger over. "If you need someone to ride on ahead, I'll be glad to do it, but that man, *nor anyone else*, is riding Badger."

As a mama bear protecting her cub, Alaina took a defiant step in front of the stallion. She did her own sizing of 'ole jingle bob' as she noted him checking Badger's attributes with narrowed eyes. She personally found the man sadly lacking. It didn't bother her one whit to let the conductor know what she thought of his solution for their situation.

She didn't even give the cowhand the time of day, ignoring him completely as she announced prophetically, "Anyway, he couldn't ride my horse. Badger wouldn't tolerate it. He would end up at the bottom of that mountain…Badger would make sure of that." Then to send home her final conclusion of the matter, she stated firmly and emphatically, "He won't allow anyone to ride him but me."

The three men exchanged looks.

With a haughty arrogance in his voice, the cowhand they called Jackson broke in, "I ain't never seen a horse I couldn't ride… 'specially a woman's horse," he retorted snidely for Alaina's benefit and then dismissed her altogether as he instructed the two men. "Jist help me git this ramp down, and I'll make that station by sundown tomorrow."

"Mister, I'm sure you are a fine horseman," Alaina began, seriously having her doubts. He had the arrogance of a man that used a whip to get the horse to do his bidding. This thought made her more determined than ever to protect her baby, standing now with hands on hips, her feet planted and firm.

Apparently these two men believed the cowhand capable of the hazardous ride or they wouldn't have suggested it. She would concede to their judgment on that matter, but it still worried her to what lengths he might go to accomplish that. No matter…they still didn't grasp the situation, apparently. "There are some fine horsemen on my father's ranch, as well, but not one of them can stay on Badger…even on flat ground."

She looked pointedly to the arrogant young cowboy and addressed him to his face. "I won't allow you to try to prove yourself a bronc rider and get broken up or killed in the process. And I *certainly* won't have you endangering my horse, either. Chances are he would injure himself on the side of that mountain just to see you fly like a bird." A hint of a mischievous grin curled the corners of her mouth as she referred to the likely fashion in which he would be ejected from the saddle.

The cowhand squared his shoulders, his eyes burning through her as he opened his mouth to speak, but the engineer raised his hand to shush him. He could tell by Alaina's demeanor that there was no use arguing. He couldn't stop the hint of a smile that he also exposed as he quickly discovered he liked her grit. "You aren't like most young girls your age. I can tell that from your spunk," he reasoned, then warned her gently, "But this is a hard country, and I don't think you know what you're takin' on."

Alaina smiled and spoke somewhat tongue-in-cheek, "You *do* know that I was born and reared in Wyoming, don't you?" she quarried. "And not just in Wyoming, but in the middle of the Rattlesnake Mountains. I've spent almost as much time under the stars as I have under a roof. This country is like home to me." She nodded with absolute certainty to the engineer, "Just point me in the right direction, and Badger and I will deliver your message for you."

The engineer seemed satisfied with that. "All right, young lady. I'll trust you to get help to us."

"This is a mistake…trusting a half-pint *girl* to get us out of this mess," the cowhand muttered to his boss.

The rancher absently shrugged. He didn't want to let on how amused he'd been by the entire exchange. This spirited young lass reminded him a lot of his brother's daughter, Victoria. Tory was a spit-fired redhead, so full of sauce there was nobody who could hope to tame her. He could tell this little lady was cut from the same cloth.

Alaina hopped down from the boxcar, glaring a warning at the young cowhand. She moved close to the rancher, quietly issuing the promise, "If he so much as touches my horse, I'll shoot him! I won't kill him," she admitted quickly, "but he'll be of no use to you for a long time to come."

He laughed outright. "I believe you would."

"Just so *he* does…"

Alaina cut a steel eye to the man in question before moving forward to the Pullman to retrieve her sheepskin coat and Stetson hat. She felt she could trust the cowhand's boss to keep him in line.

Alaina quickly retrieved a change of clothes from her trunk in the baggage car and stuffed them into her saddlebags along with a bundle of jerky she had taken from the smokehouse back at the ranch. Tossing the bags over one shoulder and her saddle over the other, she made her way back to Badger.

While she had been away, the men had lowered the ramp on the boxcar. Alaina climbed up and dropped the saddle bags at her feet. She first placed the blanket carefully in place, and then with astonishing lack of effort, she hefted the saddle up and eased it onto Badger's back. After sliding it slightly backwards and from side to side to settle it in, she tightened the cinch straps. Stooping down, she retrieved the bags and hung them behind the cantle, tying them, along with the bedroll and slicker, securely in their place with the leather latigos.

With a quiet word of encouragement and a stroke of affection for her stallion, Alaina stepped into the stirrup and swung into the saddle. She backed Badger up against the back wall of the box car and in the same instant, dug her heels into his flanks and drew air through her lips, making a loud kissing sound.

Badger took the cue and leaped toward the doorway and then sailed through the air, landing several feet down the embankment of the roadway. Without breaking stride, he half-bounded, half-slid down the mountainside to a wide shelf below. Alaina pulled him to a stop, swung him back around and waved to the men who stood spellbound beside the box car. The man in the brown suit looked down at the ground, slowly shaking his head in delighted wonder.

2. Train Wreck

The engineer had sketched out a vague map of the terrain between the location of the rockslide and the next rail station. He knew nothing of the landscape aside from the grade of the track, so he could give no advice concerning the best route by horseback. Alaina soon discovered that the shelf she was on fell away to nothing to the west, and so in order to get to the valley floor below, she would have to backtrack to the east for a bit.

For the next half hour, she allowed Badger to pick his own route downward through the boulders and fallen timber. From time to time, she caught a glimpse of the train backing slowly along the track above. Long before she reached the floor of the canyon, she began to hear rapids. She had been napping at this stage of the trip and hadn't realized the train had crossed a long trestle spanning a deep gorge.

Looking northeastward now, she could see the trestle and concluded that the rapids had to be the Humboldt River. That was a good thing. There would be game trails along the river providing a much easier route through the mountains and eventually to the rail station on the other side. She was nearing the river now and could tell that an earlier cloudburst in the higher elevations had brought it to flood stage. The roar of the rapids was now echoing in her ears, but above that, another sound caught her attention. It sounded like the train whistle.

Puzzled by the thought, she looked for a clearing that would allow her to see back up the mountain. The whistle sounded several times and then ceased, but another high-pitched screech began to echo through the canyon. When she finally found a break in the timber where the tracks were visible, she became horrified at what she saw. The train was barreling down the mountain backwards, completely out of control.

Alaina sat frozen in the saddle, looking back along the path of the track, realizing full well that the train would never make the curve onto the trestle. The screeching sound suddenly stopped. The brakes were no longer of any use to the careening locomotive. She had no way of knowing if the passengers had attempted to leap from the car before it was too late or if they were still helplessly trapped inside.

It all happened so quickly, and yet it seemed like an eternity as she sat transfixed by the scene before her, paralyzed by the inevitable outcome. She watched as the speeding train rounded the last curve before the trestle, rocking violently from side to side, wheels barely holding onto the tracks. Before the caboose had reached the center of the trestle, Alaina gasped as the entire train seemed to fold in the middle and crash through the bridge rail and into the river a hundred feet below.

*　*　*

That tragic scene had left Alaina numbed with disbelief. Finally adjusting to the reality of what she had just witnessed, she nudged Badger into a canter along the river bank toward the crash. The rough terrain made progress slow at times, requiring care and attention to maneuver around rockslides and over and around fallen timber.

Alaina estimated that hours had passed before she was actually able to see the wreckage of the train. While riding along the river, she had noticed a great deal of debris as well as personal articles from the baggage car and Pullman swirling along in the rapids. At one point, she even thought she caught a glimpse of a body, although the rolling current made it impossible to be sure.

Both banks of the river were steep and treacherous, lending no opportunity to get close to the wreckage. Sitting astride Badger atop the closest vantage point she could reach, she surveyed the wreckage and both sides of the river in an attempt to determine if there were any survivors. She could see no sign of life, only rail cars jutting from the water at various angles and depths.

She reached back into a saddlebag for binoculars. Her father had insisted she carry them with her at all times because one could never tell when the need for a closer look might arise. He had given them to her when she was fourteen, saying he realized she had reached a level of responsibility that would ensure they were appreciated and cared for properly. They were U.S. Cavalry officer issue and had belonged to her grandfather, Jamis Johnson, and passed down to her father by her grandmother.

She lifted them to her eyes and slowly moved them over the wreckage of the train and then along both sides of the river. Again, seeing no sign of life, she determined that it was no use. If anyone had survived the catastrophe, they had either jumped from the careening train or had endured the fall from the trestle and ridden the rapids down river to where they could crawl out onto a rock or shoal.

Throughout the painstaking ride back to the trestle, she had been considering what she should do next. She now had to decide. The route on across the vast Humboldt Mountain Range to the west would be treacherous, especially at this time of year. She had no way of knowing how far it was to the next rail station, and the terrain would prohibit following the tracks. Backtracking to the last station, however, would take her back across the desert. The advantage of that would be that she could use the tracks for guidance both day and night. The distance she would have to travel back home was farther than if she continued on to California, but she was more familiar with the country. She knew where the last station was and that there were watering points along the way, so her mind was made up. She gave Badger a gentle nudge and pointed him up the hill toward the end of the trestle and turned back the direction they had come.

* * *

Alaina awakened with a start. Quickly glancing around her surroundings, she realized where she was and why she was there. The painful memory of the tragic events of the day before rushed back into her head, reminding her of the urgency of her mission. She had ridden far into the night and had reached the first watering station before stopping to rest.

By her calculation, another half day's ride would bring her to the edge of the desert. She had determined to make it that far, rest until sundown, and travel across the desert sand at night. The temperature would drop drastically in the dark of the night, and both she and Badger would be able to travel farther and faster without battling the heat. Even this late in the year, the sun could become merciless, reflecting off of the desert sand. Neither of them would require as much water traveling at night, and she wasn't sure of the distance to the next water tank.

She unwrapped the bundle of jerky and placed several pieces in her coat pocket. She carried two canteens of water on her saddle, one small and one larger to allow enough for Badger. Within a few minutes, she had cleared the camp, doused the fire with the leftover coffee, packed the pan away and swung into the saddle. With a gentle nudge of her heels, she moved Badger into a slow canter along the tracks. As she had predicted, by mid-day she neared the edge of the desert wasteland she remembered from the earlier train ride. She found shelter from the sun and bedded down until evening.

* * *

The sun had moved behind the foothills to the west when Alaina once again stepped into the stirrup. The desert stretched before her like an endless ocean. The dunes were like gentle waves rolling on forever, somewhat intimidating to a young girl all alone. She had never crossed a desert by horseback, but to her recollection, it hadn't been that long of a trip by train and she had the tracks to guide her.

Badger had rested all afternoon and had been given a double portion of grain from the saddlebags. She felt his muscles ripple beneath her legs as he effortlessly moved along. A cool south breeze brushed across her face, carrying the scent of cactus and sage. It would be a long time before she would lie down again, but she was accustomed to spending days in the saddle.

She reached into her coat pocket for a piece of jerky and settled herself into the gentle rhythm of Badger's canter. Alaina chewed on the leather-like morsels as the desert sky gradually flooded with the brilliance of a multitude of stars that seemed close enough to reach out and touch. Soon a golden moon inched its way above the horizon and lit up the barren wasteland around her almost as bright as day.

Her dire predicament suddenly drained from her mind. She could easily imagine herself riding across her father's ranch back in Wyoming. The sky was the same. The moon was the same. The breeze, the fragrance, everything was as familiar as the home place where she had spent her entire life. In fact, it suddenly occurred to her that her father was more than likely looking up at the same wondrous spectacle as she was at this very moment.

Up until now, everyone would think she was still aboard the westbound train to San Francisco. There would be no reason for anyone to be concerned about her for at least two or three more days. By then, she would be able to reach a telegraph relay station and explain where she was, as well as her plans for the journey back home. Up to this point, she hadn't given much thought to the future, but she would obviously have to altar her previous plans. It would be days, possibly weeks, before the tracks would allow for regular train traffic again.

Badger had kept up the methodical pace of his gentle canter all through the night. Alaina had drifted in and out of awareness. She often caught herself slipping sideways in the saddle but was always alert enough to regain her balance. From time to time, she nibbled on jerky from her coat pocket and several times stopped to refresh Badger and herself from the canteens.

The sun rose to greet them as they pushed eastward, and the warm rays were welcomed after the long, cool night. She had thought they would stop and sit out the heat of the day in the shade of a boulder until evening, but daylight had revealed a range of mountains in the distance. Alaina had traveled across the vast expanses of Wyoming all of her life. She knew that if Badger could continue at the pace they were going, they could reach the foothills by midmorning and possibly the little township and rail station where they had last stopped by noon.

As they continued, however, storm clouds began to appear from the north, hugging the snow-covered mountain peaks and then moving across the plains. By the time they reached the foothills, a strong north wind had kicked up and snow flurries began to swirl around them, unsure of which direction they were supposed to fall. Alaina reined Badger in and untied the latigos from her oilskin slicker, pulling it on over her sheepskin coat. She removed the large bandana from around her neck, pulled it down over her hat and tied it underneath her chin.

She was glad for the rails to guide her, for she didn't need to be concerned about losing her direction. Alaina saw no need to push Badger any longer. They were steadily gaining altitude, and she felt sure they would soon reach the rail station. It would be a welcomed sight with this drastic change in the weather.

Alaina couldn't help the rush of relief she experienced as she reined Badger to a stop and inspected the sight that lay before her. The little mountain hamlet of Coalville lay stretched along one side of the tracks with the rail station on the opposite side near the center of town. As she walked Badger forward, the street was almost bare of horses or rigs, and she saw no one on the boardwalks. Before she reached the station, a movement caught her eye. She turned to look and noticed a man coming out of the sheriff's office walking toward her.

He was tall and broad through the shoulders. He wore a beard and mustache and walked with a swagger that Alaina had seen in other men—men who thought a little too highly of themselves. Somehow, he didn't seem to fit in here though, and Alaina couldn't help but wonder why such a man as he would be content to be sheriff of a little mountain village like Coalville, Utah.

By the time she had dismounted and climbed the three steps to the landing of the rail station, he had caught up to her. His voice was sharp and direct. "Young man, I need to have a word with you."

Alaina kept moving toward the door of the station. She hadn't noticed any one else crossing the street, but she felt sure the sheriff wasn't addressing her.

"Young man!"

The tone of his voice caused her to stop in her tracks, and just then she noticed her reflection in the window of the station. The sheepskin coat with the slicker pulled over it made her look much larger than she was and completely hid any girlish curves. She had pulled her hair back and pulled her hat down around her ears to shield herself against the north wind. The reflection she saw in the window showed no resemblance of a young lady.

She started to correct him, but something seemed to stop her. Perhaps being discreet about her true identity was not such a bad idea. So, instead, she tried to make her voice a bit gruffer as she spoke and kept her body turned away so as not to look directly at him.

"Yes sir, can I help you?" she responded.

"Well, yes, you can." The voice was not in the least bit friendly and carried with it a touch of mockery. "I make it my business to know who comes through my town, especially when they ride in during the middle of a storm." He took a step closer, cocking his head and narrowing his eyes to study the stranger. He had too much on the line to be taking any chances with drifters arriving in town right now. "Most people would be hunkered down to wait out the storm, so that makes me wonder where you're coming from and what your business is here in Coalville."

She did not know why, but something about this sheriff made her uneasy, and although she hadn't intended to be deceptive in the beginning, she decided to not be entirely truthful with him. "I pushed through the storm just to get here with news of a bad train accident up ahead on the tracks. A rockslide...a pretty bad one in fact, blocked the mountain pass, and when the train tried to back down the mountain, it went off into the river."

She stopped abruptly, not wanting to connect herself in any way to the location of the train as she added in a matter-of-fact tone, "I never saw it myself. The fellers who did were headed on over the mountain. Said they would inform the station on the other side and asked if I would relay the message to the station here."

She stood patiently, only allowing herself to glance sideways at the sheriff, waiting for some indication as to whether he was convinced. She had tried to express herself like someone with little or no education, but she had never been good at deception and wasn't sure she had pulled it off.

He was silent as he weighed the explanation—and the stranger. The young man would not look him in the eye, but then he'd been told he could be quite intimidating. He gave a small inward chuckle of satisfaction of that fact. It certainly had its uses from time to time. Just for the sheer personal pleasure of giving the boy an added measure of anxiety, he crossed his arms with ceremony and puffed out his chest with self-importance.

He glared at the boy for another silent moment then jerked his head in the general direction of the depot and demanded curtly, "Well, then... you better get on in there and let the ticket master know. I'm sure he'll need to telegraph the authorities and inform them."

Alaina felt her body relax and let out a slow breath of relief. She still would not look at the man. Disgust continued welling up in her at his attempt to put her in her place...or rather a poor scrawny boy in *his* place. She reminded herself that his arrogance did not matter nor his attempt to bully her. The fact that he had swallowed it all, the disguised voice and the story about the accident…that was all that mattered. She could not help but feel a bit of personal satisfaction in it, though.

Another thing, too, in that one quick encounter, she knew why the man was here—he enjoyed unrestricted power and what it could get him—and he enjoyed having control over common, ordinary people!

* * *

Pushing through the door, Alaina recognized the small man behind the ticket window. It was the same face she remembered from a few days before. She moved up before him, suddenly weary. Almost three days had passed since the horrible train wreck…with most of that time being spent in a hard, leather saddle. Finally at her destination, all the drive that had pushed her onward was gone, and Alaina felt the strength drain from her body. As she stood quietly before him, the man diligently wrote in a tally book. She had only been given a short, cursory glance by the man since she had entered.

Deciding her news was vastly more important than the man's attempt to balance his numbers, she queried flatly, "Have you been informed of a bad train wreck on up the tracks?"

With that sudden unexpected announcement, the little man's eyes jerked up filled with shock and from his lips blurted the horrified response. "No!" He then looked at her as if trying to determine if the question was truly real or if it was some atrocious joke to get his attention.

Alaina tried to hold her patience with the obtuse man as she explained sharply, "Well, there's a serious rockslide covering the tracks just over the pass, and when the train was attempting to back down the mountain, the brakes lost traction. It came barreling down the slope, and when it reached the trestle, it went through the rail and into the swollen river."

As she finished the news, her irritation with the man wavered. He stood totally still, his mouth flapping open and shut like a fish on dry land with no sound coming out. Perhaps she had been hasty and misjudged the man. He was obviously shaken, and the wide eyes and shaking hands clearly showed his distress. Alaina felt calmness inside that told her she could trust him.

She glanced back toward the door and across the room to verify that they were alone. Her voice lowered in case the walls had ears. "I wasn't entirely honest when I told the sheriff about it, but I witnessed the whole episode. I was on that train and the only person on board with a horse. I initially was going to go on over the mountain to inform the attendant at the next station about the rockslide, but when the train went into the river, I thought it best to come back this way."

She hesitated as she became overwhelmed by the recollection. Tears welled up in her eyes as she recalled all the people on the train, especially the little boy with his toy horse that he had galloped playfully up and down the aisle countless times. And then there was the young couple who were just married and going to California to begin their lives together, and the old soldier going home after many years surviving the army posts and battlefields.

She had to purposely rein in her thoughts and put the distressing memories aside for now. But the prayer that had become a litany over the last three days for the hope of survivors continued in her heart as she confessed, "I rode to the trestle and looked around for survivors with no success. I still carry hope, though, that someone could have survived."

The little man on the other side of the ticket window became transfixed by the unexpected news of such a disaster on his track. His eyes widened further in unbelief as he was finally able to splutter, "Are you serious?"

Alaina had to confront and overcome another bout of frustration with her irritation of the thick-headed man. She fought the urge to grab him by the collar and give him a good shake. The idea that he might think she was making up such a tale was ludicrous.

"Yes, sir, *quite* serious," Alaina assured him. She could not prevent her glaring reaction to his disbelief from straining her voice as she continued. "As I said, I was on the train until it reached the slide. You may remember me from our stop a few days back." As she spoke, she pulled the scarf and hat from her head, allowing her long blond hair to fall over the slicker around her shoulders.

The man's eyes popped wider in shock. "Well, I declare," he muttered. "I wouldn't have recognized you, but now, yes, I do seem to recall a young lady like you on that train." His thoughts went wild with frenzy now as he muttered under his breath, "My lord, I need to send some wires out."

With that, he spun on his heel and hurried to the telegraph key on the desk in the corner of the little room.

"When you're finished with your business, I need to send a few myself," Alaina informed him. How she longed for the luxury of the miraculous telephone. Phone lines had only recently been strung into Laramie. They were gradually spider-webbing across the west, and Alaina thought about how much more convenient it would make matters if she could speak to her mother and father instead of having to choose a few words on a piece of paper to explain her situation.

After half an hour of tapping out messages to various railroad officials, the attendant approached the window again. He took note of the weary traveler sitting quietly in the corner chair. Compassion gentled his speech, "Now young lady, who is it that you need to inform about your devastating experience? I believe it only fair and fitting that there be no charge to you for that, seeing that you've gone to such great lengths to make us aware of this tragedy."

"My mother in San Francisco and my father in Wyoming," she responded, rising from the chair to give the man the needed information.

Alaina explained to both her parents in as few words as possible where she was and that she had no choice but to return home. She assured them that she would be fine and that they shouldn't worry. She knew of course that she wasted words there. They would be extremely concerned that she would attempt to travel cross-country alone with winter coming on.

Alaina mentally calculated that she was a little over three hundred miles from Laramie and figured she could cover that in a week and a half by traveling as the crow flies even in rough terrain. She did not relish the trip, but it couldn't be helped.

"Mister," she said to the attendant, "I'd appreciate it if you wouldn't tell the sheriff about me not being honest with him. I don't know why, I just didn't feel comfortable with the way he was questioning me."

"Well, you're not the only person who feels that way," he replied. "He calls himself John Bascom. He says he's from over around Provo. He hasn't been sheriff here for long, but he has already rubbed a bunch of folks the wrong way."

The agent made his own surveillance to assure that they were alone as he glanced toward the closed door. "Between you and me, I don't know what he's doing here. Coalville was booming awhile back when the copper mine was running, but since they fell into financial difficulty, there's not a whole lot happening."

His voice hardened as he pronounced his personal convictions. "We don't need a sheriff like him. And besides that, he doesn't do much of anything but nose around asking questions about everyone in town. The mayor appointed him as sheriff without even a vote from the counsel."

The attendant tapped his temple to confirm that he had been giving the matter a lot of thought. "That seems pretty suspicious, if you ask me." Feeling he had said enough, he patted the young lady's hand that rested on the counter. "Don't you worry, though, your secret is safe with me."

Alaina smiled her thanks and nodded her appreciation. She twisted her hair back into a ball, shoved it underneath her hat again and pulled the brim back down, tying it with her scarf.

"Can you direct me to the nearest stable? I need to see to my horse," she inquired.

"Sure can, miss." He pointed toward the north. "Down at the edge of town and on your left. You can't miss it. We don't have a hotel, but there's a boarding house just back this way a bit from the stable. You won't have trouble finding it."

"Thank you, sir, I appreciate it." Alaina gave him a weary smile as she closed the door and moved to Badger.

The attendant walked to the window to watch her mount the magnificent animal. His heart tripped a bit as the stallion side-stepped and tossed his head, letting out a snort that he heard all the way in the office. He took pleasure in watching the sight of the two of them moving down the street, secretly feeling some regret that he was not her age again and a little more aggressive in personality. Blushing at the absurdity of the thought, he turned back to the dreaded task before him. He had to go through the list of names and compile a directory of possible victims of the accident.

With a heavy sigh, he practically fell into the chair that Alaina had just vacated; the duty struck him as being almost overwhelming.

3. A Mother's Instinct

Attorney Catherine Johnson ached to drop her head on the top of her cluttered desk in frustration and dismay. The stacks and stacks of papers were driving her insane. She was a very organized, structured person, and the research and forms required for this case were astronomical to say the least.

She wanted to push the paper mountain off into the floor out of her sight, but then she would just have a mess to clean up with no hope of getting them in the right order…besides, she was not given to the throwing of tantrums as much as she desired to have a small fit. She was very dignified and refined, just ask anyone—anyone except her Pawpaw and her husband. But, of course, *they* did not count! They were emotionally biased.

If the schedule went according to plan, Alaina would be arriving in just a few more days on the westbound train, and Cat would have much needed help. She knew it would not be a chore her daughter relished, but Alaina was dependable and exceptionally responsible for a girl of her young age. Until she arrived, however, Cat was stuck with the heavy workload.

With a sigh of resignation, she decided it was time for a break and an afternoon walk to clear her head. She thought perhaps a stroll down to the general store for a chocolate bar would be a good idea. Chocolate was a newly discovered miraculous cure for all kinds of ailments, and Cat quickly realized that the need for a miraculous cure came more and more frequently the longer this case continued. With this decision made, she felt better already as she stood and reached for her bonnet.

Although her presence in San Francisco had been unsolicited and unexpected, it had afforded her familiarity with the people and businesses in the area. She had been on a first name basis with many of her daily acquaintances, especially the general store owner and chocolate salesman, Neal Baker. The hustle and bustle of the city of San Francisco was a great deal different from the peace and solitude of the Wyoming wilderness. The novelty of city life had quickly lost its luster!

Cat kept an eagle-eye out for the bicyclers...especially the young ones. She had quickly decided that they must have some kind of death wish. They were everywhere! She found herself intrigued by the contraption but inwardly kept a vow that if she straddled anything that moved, it would breathe, have four legs and a warm hairy body. She had studied the spindly, spoke wheels with distrust. They kept you upright only by one's own balance, and Cat would be the first to admit that she sometimes had trouble just remaining upright on her feet on level ground, let alone astraddle a two-wheeled gizmo. Give her a long day in a saddle anytime!

She started to step across the tracks but suddenly jumped backward, quickly glancing this way and that to make sure there were no cable cars barreling down on her. Her sigh was audible. Oh, how she longed for the sleepy solace of home!

Quickly crossing the tracks, she walked across the brick-paved street. She had pondered more than once about the bricks. She supposed it would be nice not to have to walk on a muddy street when it rained. Cat knew first-hand how messy that could be. It rarely rained in Wyoming, but it never rained in California! Were it not for the vast web of irrigation ditches crisscrossing the valleys, the place would be the next thing to desert.

She shook her head in disdain, confirming within herself for the thousandth time that city-dwellers were astonishingly weak and spoiled! *These poor folks wouldn't survive one winter in Wyoming,* she thought to herself.

Neal Baker looked up from his task of replenishing the shelves with canned goods when the door opened. His smile came easy. The woman entering his store was not only a pleasure to look at, but he never tired of her stories of life out in the wilderness. "Good afternoon, Mrs. Cat."

"Afternoon, Neal. How is business today?"

He turned to the box setting on the counter. Lifting the lid, he removed a bar of Swiss chocolate from within. He laid it before the woman without ceremony. "Much better now."

She grinned as she reached thankfully for the sweet treat. "Careful, Neal. Missy will get jealous."

"Awe, Missy knows where her place is." He patted the center of his chest with a sly grin.

"She's a very lucky lady."

"She surely is...and I tell her often enough that she won't forget, either."

Cat laughed freely. It felt good. The stress of the day melted away, but for the life of her, she could not quite put aside this irritating nagging in the pit of her stomach. She did not know what the problem was, but for the past three days, there had been this uncomfortable sensation in her gut that something was amiss.

She always enjoyed her visits with Neal and his petite wife, Missy, so Cat deliberately concentrated on having a pleasant talk with her friend. "I'm sure she knows without having to be reminded."

"Yes, but a bit of reminding never hurt anybody," he declared seriously, wagging his finger in front of her face as if expounding his point, though Cat caught the mischievous twinkle in his eyes.

She carefully unwrapped the chocolate bar as if the delayed action would make the sweet delight all the more pleasurable. As she broke off one end and slowly placed it on her tongue, her eyes slid closed as the burst of sweet flavor seemed to fill her very soul. She sighed as she softly exclaimed, "Okay, I think I can survive the rest of the day."

Cat freely offered the bar out for Neal to break off a bite. He shook his head. "Naw, you look like you need the whole thing today."

"I miss home. I'm not used to being gone so long," Cat admitted, breaking off a chunk herself and handing it to the man. *And not used to my gut twisting in knots over something that I can't figure out!* she finished silently to herself.

Neal reluctantly took the offering but, unlike Cat, he popped it into his mouth quickly enough. "Well, I, for one, will miss you when you go. Missy will, too."

"Well, it won't be for good I'm afraid," she responded laughingly. "I'm getting more and more offers to come to the West Coast these days."

"You should just move here and be done with it."

She was quick to shake her head. "Oh, no! Never!" Her smile was gentle. "My heart is in Wyoming."

"Talk that man of yours into coming to California for a spell. There's opportunities aplenty."

"Tall would feel so closed in he couldn't breathe. He's even worse than me when it comes to the city."

He patted her hand in comfort. "Well, maybe before long you can go back home."

She nodded. "My daughter, Alaina, will be arriving soon. She'll be a tremendous help, and hopefully we can wrap this case up without any more delay."

With just the mention of her name, Cat felt a wave of nausea wash over her. *What in the world is wrong with me?* she demanded inwardly. She suddenly felt the need to have her daughter in her arms and in her sight so that she could confirm that Alaina was alright. Two days could not pass quickly enough!

"I look forward to meeting her."

Cat forced herself to smile, taking a deep, calming breath. "You'd better put in another order for that Swiss chocolate. There'll be two of us coming to visit."

"It's already on its way," he informed her cunningly.

She laughed as she dug into her purse to pay for the chocolate bar. "I need to get some lotion, also. And I'm out of the scented talcum that Missy put me on to. I'll have to start stocking up so I can take a good supply of it home with me."

"That will give you a good reason to come back sometime," he announced as he began to collect her purchases.

"I think I've had enough of the big city to last me a lifetime…but I've made some good friends here." Her smile indicated that she included Neal in that group.

"Well, we're honored to know you, too, Cat Johnson."

"Thanks, Neal. I feel likewise." She confirmed as she took her box of supplies and handed him payment, with a little extra. "I'll probably be seeing you tomorrow, and you keep whatever is left over."

"I'll look for you, and thanks, but you shouldn't do that," he returned with a half wave.

Cat nodded with a departing wave of her own as she moved out to the boardwalk, snapping the door shut behind her.

Suddenly she clutched her stomach as if she had been caught blindsided and punched in the gut. She leaned backward against the door, the smile dying instantly on her face.

Something was wrong!

"Alaina?" she whispered almost quizzically under her breath.

Cat could barely stand as she pushed away from the building. Her legs trembled, and her hands were shaking so badly she could hardly hold on to the box of supplies. Her eyes snapped up toward the telegraph office as she immediately began making a beeline for the building.

She rushed through the door, clutching the box with a death grip. "Please…I need to send a telegraph. It's urgent."

The operator frowned at the pale woman standing before the counter. "Yes ma'am." He quickly grabbed a paper and pulled the pencil from the top of his ear. He dabbed the lead end with his tongue a few times. "Okay, I'm ready. Who to?"

"Tall Johnson at Wells Flats, Wyoming," she informed him quickly. "I need to know if Alaina boarded the train and is coming to California as planned."

Jotting down the information, the operator moved to tap away the message. He glanced worriedly at the frantic woman. He returned, wanting to offer some reassurance. "The message is sent."

Cat frowned up at him with worry. "Is the train on schedule?"

"It is as far as I know, ma'am. We haven't heard differently." He nodded to the line of chairs against the wall. "You can wait if you like. It may take some time for a reply, but I can see this is important to you."

"Yes, thank you," Cat murmured.

Instead of sitting, however, she set the box from the store on a chair and began to pace. Time seemed to drag on for an eternity. The sun was sinking when the reply finally came. With the first tap of the telegraph key, Cat rushed up to the counter. It was all she could do to refrain from screaming at the man to hurry and tell her the message.

He handed her the paper, vocally confirming what the paper said. "She's on the train."

He suddenly turned back toward the telegraph key board as the tapping started again.

Cat moved to the chairs, unable to stand any longer. She still felt that nagging, horrible, sick feeling inside…the inward sense that something was wrong. Something had happened to Alaina! She was somewhere between Wyoming and California alone on a train, and something was wrong.

Cat knew her daughter could take care of herself, but the wilderness was very unforgiving and harsh. Travel through the mountains was dangerous in the best of circumstances. No one knew that fact better than her husband. Tall's father, Jamis Johnson, had perished out in the wilderness, and he was a grown man accustomed to weathering the elements.

Her troubled thoughts were interrupted as the attendant called out, "Ma'am, I have another message addressed to you, and it's from Alaina Johnson."

Cat bounded out of the chair, instantly running to the counter. Her fists were clinched as she demanded. "What did she say?"

He looked at her gravely, but instantly reassured her, "She's okay, but there was a terrible accident. The train went off the tracks, and it seems that your Alaina is the only survivor."

Cat clutched both fists against her chest, her heart pounding. "What does the message say…every word of it?"

4. A Call for Compassion

Alaina settled Badger into a stall at the livery and walked the short distance back to the boarding house. The one room that was available was upstairs. It was small with only a half bed, but the chimney from the fireplace below came up through the outside wall, keeping it toasty warm. She was thankful for the window overlooking the street, and before lighting the lantern, she peaked through the curtain to see if anyone was moving outside.

She could not put her finger on it, but something made her very uneasy about this place. There was no activity along either boardwalk, so she washed up and laid out the other change of clothes she had brought along. Her thoughts immediately went back to her trunk in the baggage car.

Wonder where all of my personals ended up? she mused.

She caught herself and realized how insensitive the thought was and how grateful that she wasn't there with it, wherever *it* was. For the first time, she came to grips with how close she had come to dying. Had it not been for her insistence upon bringing Badger along, she would have been on the train with all of the other passengers when it went into the river.

Before she stretched out on the bed, she placed the one straight-backed chair in the room underneath the doorknob and wedged it tightly in place. Her dad had instilled into her head that one should always do everything possible to protect oneself, no matter what it was about. Perhaps the chair was not necessary, but she was going to take every precaution! The bed was anything but comfortable, but her tired body welcomed it.

* * *

Alaina awoke suddenly, realizing someone was at the door. In the faint glow from the window, she could see the knob twisting one way and then the other. She had secured the deadbolt, and the chair remained wedged in place. Someone would have to really want in to break through both the deadbolt and the chair.

Her saddle gun was leaning against the bed frame and the wall. She reached for it as she slid silently onto the floor and backed to the far corner of the room. She jacked a cartridge into the chamber as loudly as she could.

"Whoever is at the door," she began in the huskiest voice she could muster, afraid the unwanted visitor could hear the furious pounding of her heart. "You're lucky I don't empty this rifle into your middle. Were I you, I'd find me another place to be right now!"

She heard floorboards creaking as someone moved back to the stairway. She went to the window and waited, peering through the curtain to the boardwalk below. Sure enough, after several minutes, a figure of a large man appeared and hugged close to the storefronts as he hurried along the walkway. She thought she recognized the swagger but couldn't be sure because of his haste.

There was no way to tell the time, but Alaina felt rested and thought she must have slept several hours. She felt reasonably sure there would be no more unexpected visits. She lay back down but sleep would not come, so she decided to be on her way before daylight.

She dressed hurriedly, gathered up her rifle and saddle bags and crept quietly down the stairs. Looking both ways down the boardwalk, she felt satisfied that no one was on the street, so she moved quickly toward the livery. Badger nickered softly as she entered the stable. She took the time to brush him down before placing the blanket and saddle on him. She did not know how far they may have to travel before he would be pampered again.

Once more, she checked the street. Seeing no one, she led Badger out, fastened the door and swung into the saddle. The snow-covered street muffled the hoof beats as horse and rider disappeared into the early morning darkness. When they cleared the edge of the little mountain town, Alaina nudged Badger into a gentle canter. The more distance she could put between herself and that sheriff, the better she would feel.

The sun was indicating about noon when Alaina eased Badger into a walk. She guessed they had traveled at least twenty miles. The morning had brought a welcomed change in the weather. The sun came up in a clear sky. A gentle breeze had kicked up from the south, and soon the snow had disappeared. Alaina knew that if anyone had been attempting to follow, the melting snow would foil any chance of their success, for Badger's tracks would melt away with it.

They had crossed a wide, plain-like valley into the foothills of another range of mountains which Alaina thought to be the Uintas. If she was correct in her assumption, they would stretch into Southwestern Wyoming, and by tomorrow she could at least be back in her home state. She would still be a few hundred miles from Laramie, but the thought of being back in Wyoming gave her a warm, comforting feeling.

She pointed Badger toward a steep escarpment of red rocks she had spied from a distance, thinking that it looked like a probable place to find water. Not that she needed any for drinking purposes, but she thought she might wash out the stale clothes in her saddlebag and take advantage of the warm noonday sun to hurriedly dry them. It would be nice to find a young rabbit or squirrel to roast over a fire, as well.

As she drew closer, she could see that there were some large cottonwood trees along the base of the cliff. *That's a good sign for water,* she thought with satisfaction.

She let Badger choose his way through the sage, wanting to let him cool down completely before they stopped for a rest. He soon pushed through the last wall of brush onto the grassy bank of a shallow, but swift, running stream. The brook was clear and cold, and Alaina allowed Badger to move to the center of the current and drink from the cool, refreshing, mountain spring water. Brookie trout raced away in both directions, disturbed by their presence.

She pulled Badger's head up after a few gulps, being careful not to let him drink too much all at once. She was about to take him across to the other side when she noticed something next to the water's edge downstream a way. She could not tell for sure what it was, but it looked much like a man's body.

A chill moved down her spine as she thought of the possibility that she was not alone here. She jerked her head around, swiftly scanning the area, realizing she had been careless when she rode in. She had just not expected to cross paths with anyone this far from any settlement. She quickly looked up and down the stream again for any other sign of life. She saw no one, but still not satisfied, she pulled Badger around and went back the way they had come.

Using the line of trees and brush along the stream for cover, she moved downstream toward the heap she had spied beside the water. When she reached a point that she calculated to be close to the area, she eased out of the saddle and dropped the reigns to the ground, knowing Badger wouldn't budge until she came for him or whistled for him to come to her.

Pulling her saddle gun from the scabbard, she crept to the edge of the underbrush. Sure enough, it was a body all right! Judging from the appearance from where she crouched beside a cottonwood tree, whoever was laying on that rocky slope was dead.

Alaina swung around with her back against the tree trunk, tossing her head aside and squeezing her eyes tightly shut to take away the image. She'd never seen a dead body before! Not out in the wilderness, anyway. She'd been to funerals, of course, but the top of the box had usually been nailed shut already. True, she'd seen a couple of real corpses, but they were both old people and laid out on a bed...all freshly washed and covered with a colorful patchwork quilt as if someone had just tucked them into bed for the night.

It was nothing like this raw carnage she had just witnessed!

She listened intently for any sound that might indicate movement around her. For several minutes she sat still and totally quiet, trying to steady her breathing and calm her frantically pounding heart. She neither heard nor saw any movement, and after a few minutes, she could hear the birds begin chattering and whistling in the treetops. She knew they would not have returned to the area if there were any activity in the vicinity.

Taking a deep breath to steady her nerves, Alaina pushed upright and away from the cottonwood. Her eyes surveyed the channel of the stream in both directions for any movement. Finally convinced that she was in no immediate danger, she crept through the water to the other side of the stream.

After another deep breath to prepare herself for what she might see, Alaina rolled the body over for a closer look. She inhaled sharply at the sight, suddenly feeling the urge to be sick. The poor soul lying at her feet had been beaten mercilessly.

She squinted at the face, forcing herself to ignore the horrendous sight and take note of the features. She was not sure, but she thought it was a young Mexican girl. Her face had been bruised and cut open by constant pounding of fists or some other blunt object. Her eyes were swollen shut and black and blue. Blood caked every inch of her skin that was not covered by clothing. Her hair was matted with a mixture of blood and dirt.

Saddened by the site before her, Alaina moved a few feet away to sit on a large rock at the water's edge. She sorrowfully looked on the girl and mourned. She could not comprehend how someone could be so vicious and cruel toward another person. She just did not understand…and knew she never would.

Weary of pondering about the cruelty of men, Alaina looked around for a suitable place away from the water for a burial site. She waded back across the shallow stream and fell against Badger. She desperately needed the touch of something living. She ached for her family and could not wait to be home. She pressed her wet cheeks against Badger's neck and threw her arms around him.

"Such a waste, Badger…such a waste!" she cried.

Badger let out a soft whinny, tossing his head at the sound of her voice.

Roughly raking the back of her hands across her eyes, Alaina deliberately wiped away the tears and stepped back to caress his neck. "You're right, boy. We need to get moving."

Dreading the task before her, Alaina led Badger up next to the body. With a deep, steadying breath, she reached underneath the girl's shoulders to lift her up, and as she began to raise her from the ground, she thought she heard something. A faint moan, possibly.

Her breath caught in surprise as she trained her eyes on the young face for confirmation. *Surely not!* she thought.

She paused for a moment, and there it was again! Yes, it was a definite sound…and since it did not come from her or Badger, it must have been the poor soul in her arms! She eased the young girl back to the ground and quickly pulled her scarf from around her neck as she moved to the water. Her eyes glanced back to the girl as she hastily dunked the material in the cold mountain stream and rushed back to her. She began to carefully bathe the young girl's face, offering soft, comforting words she was not sure if the girl could hear or not.

Some form of consciousness began to return, and with it a series of moans and mutterings that Alaina could not understand. She retrieved her canteen from her saddle horn and periodically poured a few drops into the girl's mouth, not wanting her to get an upset stomach on top of her other troubles. From her mutterings and moaning, it soon became clear to Alaina that the girl was not speaking English, and Alaina knew very little Spanish.

She did not know how bad her condition was, but Alaina knew she couldn't leave this poor girl here alone. She was convinced that they were a long way from a doctor, and if she were to have a chance to live through this, it would be up to Alaina to make it happen. Quickly she began to work out a plan. First, they would need shelter, and she couldn't find shelter just sitting here. The girl desperately needed her help, but they both needed protection from the elements.

With a despairing request for the girl to stay alive, she clasped her hand and gave it an encouraging squeeze. "Stay with me…please, stay with me," she muttered.

She covered the girl with her slicker to protect her from the biting wind and jumped for a stirrup. She nudged Badger into a brisk canter farther down the stream. After covering a mile or more, not finding what she was looking for, she swung him around and went back the other direction. After passing the girl and traveling upstream, the mountains began to close in.

Soon Alaina found herself in a narrow canyon with a small stream flowing along its floor. Looking ahead, it seemed as if it ended in a sheer cliff, but as she drew nearer, she realized the canyon curved around, and right in its bend, the stream had carved out a cave-like overhang. Not the best, but it would do for now.

Alaina rode back to the girl in a dead run. She felt a bit guilty pushing Badger so ruthlessly, but she knew she must hurry or darkness would come upon them before she was prepared.

Alaina always carried extra leather latigos in her saddle bag. Her father had taught her to do that from childhood, *for one could never tell what need might arise*, he had said. They had come in handy on several previous occasions. This time it was for tying poles together to fashion a travois. She had never made one, but she had seen many, and the main objective was to make it hold together well enough to carry the intended load and stay attached to the animal you wished to pull it. Pretty simple, really. Now the challenge was to make it work!

After what seemed like hours of trial and error, she felt that she had accomplished her mission. She lashed the poles to the 'D' ring on each side of her saddle, and with some effort, she rolled the girl onto the platform she had made with sticks and her bedroll. She climbed aboard, and with feet in the stirrups, legs squeezing against the poles and gripping them with her hands, she nudged Badger slowly along the floor of the canyon.

The sun had set, and darkness began to settle into the canyon as she tried to make the girl comfortable underneath the overhang. She soon had a fire going with water heating in the small pan from the saddlebag. It would not be a fancy meal tonight, but the small pieces of jerky simmering in a pan over the coals would make a nutritious broth for the girl.

* * *

For several hours Alaina tended her unexpected patient, bathing her wounds and periodically spooning the jerky broth through her swollen lips. She carried no form of disinfectant or medication in her saddlebag, but she located a White Birch tree nearby and used the inner bark to make a poultice for the worst cuts and bruises. She used the water she had boiled it in to bathe the rest of the girl's injuries.

Her father had spent several years with the Shoshone when he was a young boy and had forever been subjecting everyone around him to the natural healing methods he had learned from the natives. Alaina was thankful now that she had recalled what he had taught her about the healing properties of the White Birch tree.

At some point during the night, she drifted into a half-conscious trance. She was so weary and spent from the emotional and physical strain of the last few days but the soft mutterings of the young Mexican girl brought her fully awake as dawn began to break.

She followed the ritual of the previous evening, preparing broth and poultice and bathing her wounds, and soon the girl was resting quietly. Alaina knew that the healing process was not going to be swift. In fact, closer scrutiny had revealed severe swelling in both arms and one thigh. Alaina had no medical training, but she had read in news articles and journals that swelling could indicate broken bones. The injuries were too old for her to even consider trying to set the breaks. They would have to be left to chance. That bothered her tremendously, for she wanted desperately to see the young girl recover from this.

Something else that bothered her was the time factor. She needed to be traveling, but to move her newly acquired patient would surely be fatal to her. She thought about going back to Coalville for help, but it would mean leaving the girl alone for a full day's time, unable to even provide herself with a drink of water.

Then there was the unpleasant feeling in her stomach at the remembrance of the town sheriff. Something told her she would be wise to steer clear of that man. She had no conception of the distance to any settlements or towns in any direction. Another troublesome thought was her parents. She knew they would be worried about her, but she saw no alternative but to hole up here until the girl could be moved, and that meant no contact with her folks for a while.

The thought of 'holing up here' snapped Alaina to attention. She looked around her at the makeshift shelter. It was accommodating enough for one or two nights but certainly not for any lengthy stay. Her first and most pressing duty would be to find or prepare a more permanent place of abode. After caring for the girl again and making sure she was sound asleep once more, she saddled Badger and began a very intense quest for a more adequate campsite.

Riding upstream, she discovered that the canyon widened out. The stream became smaller as she passed little tributary brooks and springs that fed it. Often, she would leave the main canyon to scout smaller ones leading off on both sides. After several hours, she became restless to be back with the young girl and was near giving up when she discovered a tributary that ran down through an arroyo that led northward. There were large boulders along both sides with tall pines almost completely covering the entire canyon.

She reined Badger northward into the little tributary stream and wound in and out through the giant boulders and tall pines. She had gone only a short distance when she found what she was looking for, a gaping hole in the side of the mountain with a little trickle of water running from the mouth and down into the little brook she had been following.

Closer investigation proved it to be even better than she had hoped. Large boulders piled against the cliff of the mountain formed a cave-like room large enough to make a comfortable dwelling. Water seeped from the back wall of the cliff and formed a pool in the floor before trickling through the opening and down to the brook.

All the comforts of home, Alaina thought to herself. *It's secluded, shielded from the weather, and low enough altitude that deep snow wouldn't pose a problem.*

She would make the move tomorrow.

On the return trip to camp, Alaina spied a Blue Grouse perched high in a spruce right up next to the trunk. Her appetite was definitely ready for something other than jerky, and a real broth would be an excellent remedy to strengthen the young Mexican girl.

Slipping her saddle gun from its scabbard, she took careful aim. A single, well-placed shot from the lever action forty-five caliber brought the grouse tumbling to the ground with its head missing.

Haven't lost my touch, she thought, as she retrieved the bird and placed it in the saddle bag.

Several days went by with a remarkably similar schedule for Alaina. After moving into the cave, her priority had been tending her patient with the utmost care. During the periods when the girl was resting peacefully, Alaina made sure they were well-supplied with camp meat. Her experience with dressing and preparing the good Lord's bounty reached all the way back to her early childhood days. Her dad had instructed her carefully on the importance of caring for fresh meat properly so it would not spoil.

She recalled going on hunts with him from the beginning of her memory. The highlight had always been the time she watched him bring down a buffalo. Buffalo had become more and more scarce on the western plains, and after that one last bull, her dad refused to kill any more, saying they could eat venison or antelope or even beef, and that the day might very well come when the American Bison would be completely gone.

But to a little girl, this one occasion of seeing that great, magnificent, wooly animal up close, and even perching astraddle on top of it before the skinning process began, was indelibly burned into her memory. Even now, when she entered her father's private study room, that very buffalo skin rug stretched across the floor and carried her back with a flood of memories to all the wonderful carefree days of riding with her dad across the endless expanse of the high plains of Wyoming in a quest for the bounty nature had to offer.

The canyon below and the surrounding hills where she had first camped were rich with game, so their menu was ever changing with truly little time required for hunting. Alaina decided to close off part of the opening of their dwelling to give more protection from the wind and snow. Rocks of all sizes and shapes were plentiful, and she soon learned that she had an uncanny knack for fitting them together to form a solid wall. When she was finished, there was only a small opening for a doorway.

Throughout the project, she had taken timeouts to prepare broth and poultices for the many injuries that covered the young girl's body. Alaina saw marked improvement in the healing process in her patient, despite the constant tearful mumblings and fitful half comatose state she remained in. Alaina had immobilized the broken limbs as best she could, but for the past few days renewed strength had brought on much more movement from the young girl, and Alaina feared she would reinjure them.

She had finished with her evening meal and sat waiting for the girl to stir so she could give her water and more broth when she heard someone speak. Although she did not understand the words, just the sound of words spoken with clarity startled her. She turned to see if some stranger had crept into the camp, only to find the young girl looking at her from her makeshift bed of pine boughs and blankets.

"*Donde estoy,*" the girl mumbled.

"I'm sorry," Alaina responded, "What did you say?"

"*Donde estoy,*" she repeated weakly.

"I don't understand," Alaina tried to explain. "*No entiendo.*" She thought she had heard her dad use that word when trying to communicate with Mexican traders from Colorado.

The girl moved her eyes around the cave with a questioning expression and immediately Alaina caught on. "You're safe here," she assured her with a wide smile, wishing she had paid more attention to the few Spanish lessons her mother had insisted she have.

"English?" Alaina questioned. "Do you speak English?" The girl moved her head from side to side ever so slightly. *Oh boy,* Alaina thought to herself, *this is going to be more difficult than I realized.*

At least she was finally conscious now. That was a great improvement and gave Alaina some consolation that her healing technique was working.

5. THE SEARCH

Tall Johnson rolled out of bed before dawn, as was his custom, and went directly to the big wood-burning cook stove in the kitchen. He opened the door to the firebox and raked the coals with a small poker to sift the ashes through the grate. Retrieving half a dozen sticks of stove wood from the rack, he laid them on the red-hot embers and left the door cracked open to allow air to circulate enough to fan them into flames in short order.

By the time he had thrown together makings for a pot of strong coffee, the crackling fire told him he could close the door and go about his early chores. He pulled on his coat and reached for his old Stetson hat as he headed for the barn. Concho nickered softly as he opened the barn door, indicating he was ready for his morning feeding. Tall poured grain into his feed pan and took the time to give him a good brushing while he ate.

He noticed that the once black mane and tail had faded to gray and white over the years. He didn't know Concho's exact age but estimated he had to be at least thirty. Fairly old for a horse, Tall noted, but he was still in good health and still able to produce some of the best foals on the ranch. Tall was selective about the mares he paired him with now, though.

When the bottom of the feed pan had been licked clean, he pushed the door open to the stall and led the way to the paddock that had been Concho's home since Tall first brought him to the old homestead over twenty years ago. The sun was just peaking through the trees, promising a fine Wyoming autumn day as they entered the paddock.

He moved to Concho's shoulder and wrapped his arms around the big gray's neck as he did every morning before leaving him to go about the duties of the day. Concho responded by reaching his head around Tall's body with what his wife, Cat, called a horsey hug. Tall smiled as he thought about Cat. He missed her terribly. When she left for San Francisco, she had only intended to be gone for a few weeks, but weeks had become months, and there seemed to be no end to the court case she was involved in.

To make matters worse, the request had come for Alaina to join her there, leaving Tall all alone in the big ranch house. Alaina had been gone over a week now, and the growing uneasiness in his gut that had begun the day he received a telegram about a train accident and Alaina's plans to travel back home alone had grown with each passing day.

Had he been given the opportunity, he would have objected to her decision to travel three hundred miles across wild country alone with winter coming on. He knew, however, that his objection would probably not have changed Alaina's mind about it. She had been blessed with a double dose of independence and stubbornness from both her parents.

Tall had returned to the kitchen and poured himself a hot cup of coffee as he continued musing over the situation. He knew Alaina was well able to take care of herself, but every day that passed without a word about her progress made the knot in his stomach grow bigger and tighter.

He rose suddenly from the table where he had only just sat down. A new determination quickened his steps as he threw provisions together for several days on the trail and hurried out to find the ranch foreman to instruct him to see after things until his return. Immediately he knew his decision was late in coming. This caused him to feel upset with himself, and he found himself longing to already be in Coalville, Utah, the town from where Alaina had sent the telegram.

Tall wasted no time in preparation for his journey. His bedroll, saddlebag, and slicker remained intact with his saddle year-round. Weather in Wyoming was never predictable, and he was forever finding himself in situations where he needed to be away from the ranch headquarters overnight. Thus, he tried to remain prepared for a night out under the stars at all times.

The young gray mare he had chosen from his personal remuda seemed to somehow sense the urgency in his movement as he led her from the barn. She was already moving out in a gentle canter as Tall swung his leg over to settle into the saddle. She was Tall's favorite pick of all of Concho's recent offspring and was foaled by one of Tall's best mares. He had named her Sassy because of her independence from birth and her insolent nature toward her mother.

Tall remembered how as a baby she would demand to nurse, and when the mare wasn't quick enough to oblige, she would turn her little rump to her and pound her rib cage with her tiny hooves until her mother gave in to her wishes. Her independent attitude was a fine quality in a saddle horse. She seemed to care less about being with other horses. She rather liked the company of her man.

In less than an hour, Sassy's long steady gait covered the distance to the little settlement that had sprung up around the trading post. Folks in the area had begun calling it Wells Flats. It seemed fitting since Roy Wells had built the trading post that started it all.

He pointed Sassy toward the livery stable, and when she approached the hitch rail, he stepped down and draped the reins over, not bothering to tie them. He knew that nothing or no one could budge her from that place until he returned, a trait he instilled in all of his saddle horses.

A middle-aged man wearing a leather apron peered at him from the blacksmith shop next door. "Howdy, Tall," he greeted, waving a pair of tongs. "Fine looking animal ye got there."

"Good morning, Pete," Tall shot back over his shoulder as he moved toward the stage depot, allowing the compliment to go unnoted. He pushed hurriedly through the door, finding the room empty except for the young man who doubled as the ticket master for the stage line and agent for Western Union.

"Mornin', Mr. Johnson," the young man offered as he peeked over a pair of horn-rimmed spectacles.

"Jens," Tall acknowledged with a nod, "Do you happen to know the whereabouts of Sheriff Frost this morning?" Everyone called him Jens. His name was really Harvey Jenson, although Tall could never remember anyone calling him by his first name.

"No sir," the young man replied, rising from his chair. "I haven't heard a peep out o' him this morning. He headed out to Medicine Bow late yestidy but didn't say when he planned to come back over this way."

"Well, I need to find him in a hurry!" Tall exclaimed, tamping down the anxiety that wouldn't go away. "Would you get on that telegraph key and see if he's still there?"

"Sure thing, Mr. Johnson," he responded, while sitting back in his chair.

"I'll be over at the mercantile if you hear anything right away," Tall added, already heading for the door.

Roy Wells had added on to both sides of the original log building that had been the trading post. After the addition, he placed a big sign up over the front that read *Wells' Mercantile.*

Roy looked up from assisting a customer as Tall entered. A near smile curled the corners of his mouth as he spoke. "Hey there, Tall," he greeted. "What ya been up to these days?"

"No good," Tall responded. "No good at all. Waiting to find out where Sheriff Frost is. I'm about to head for Utah if I don't have word from that girl of mine within the next few hours." He couldn't stop the worried frown creasing his forehead as he shook his head in frustration. He was still agitated with himself for taking so long to make a move in rectifying the situation. "Something must have gone wrong for her not to inform me of her progress. She should have made it to Laramie two days ago, and I should have already been out looking for her when I didn't hear from her."

"Well, I wouldn't get all worked up just yet," Roy comforted. "You know how these young 'uns are. Shoot, she may be in Laramie as we speak and just hadn't thought about you worrying. That girl has been an independent lass since she was two," he finished with a chuckle.

"Two?" Tall responded, questioningly. "I could agree if you hadn't completed the thought. She became independent at the age of about two days." Tall moved up to the man, worry in the tone. "But it isn't like her to be irresponsible. She would have sent her mother and me an update every few days when there was telegraph lines available."

He shook away the nagging fear for his young daughter, tending to the business that would get him out there looking for her. "I'm going to need a couple of pounds of jerky, a pound of coffee and a box of forty-five cartridges."

Roy had just finished putting Tall's order on the counter when Jens entered the mercantile and walked toward the two men.

"Sheriff Frost is still in Medicine Bow and says if you need him, he'll be back tomorrow," Jens reported.

Tall shook his head at the man, replying, "Send a wire back and tell him to stay put until I get there, and I'll meet him at the hotel sometime this evening."

Jens spun on his heel and hurried out the door. Tall collected the articles from the counter, bid goodbye to Roy and returned to the livery to pack the things away for the trip.

Jens stepped out onto the boardwalk of the depot. "I sent the message, Mr. Johnson," he shouted.

"Thanks, Jens. Say, if you get a gram for me from my daughter, Alaina, I need for you to forward it to me. I'll be in Medicine Bow tonight and Rawlins tomorrow. After that, I'll be taking the train to Coalville, Utah. From Coalville, I'll backtrack all the way to Laramie looking for her. Do you have all of that?" Tall questioned.

"Yes, Sir…got it down," Jens answered as he jotted a note on a piece of folded paper and stuck it into his pocket.

Tall threw the reigns around Sassy's neck and stepped for the stirrup. In a matter of minutes, Wells Flats was shrinking away in the distance behind them.

* * *

The main street of Medicine Bow was almost deserted as Tall rode up to the Hotel. Darkness had settled in early due to a covering of dark clouds that had sped in from the northwest. A north wind had kicked up and caused the temperature to drop suddenly. Tall had reached for his oilskin slicker an hour earlier, thinking how glad he was that the wind was at his back.

He recognized Sheriff Marc Frost's mount at the hitch rail even before he drew near enough to make out the small C/T brand on his left shoulder. The black gelding Marc called Hermes had turned his tail to the wind and stood lazily with one back foot resting on the front edge of the hoof as if he planned on being there for a while. Hermes was also an offspring from Concho. Tall had made sure Sheriff Frost was provided with fine mounts throughout his years as sheriff.

Recently Sheriff Marc Frost had taken after his school teacher father and had begun reading up on ancient history. He had said that Hermes was the Greek god of travel and the messenger of the gods. What better handle could there be for his black steed? Tall smiled as he remembered.

Tall found Marc seated in the hotel café and prepared to plant himself in the chair across the table. Marc smiled up at him without saying anything. Tall had long become accustomed to his mischievous nature and held his silence in an attempt to torture the longtime friend, for he could tell that curiosity was eating him alive.

Marc could finally stand it no longer. "Okay, what's so almighty important that it couldn't wait 'till I got back tomorrow?" he quizzed.

Tall's demeanor suddenly changed. "It's Alaina. I haven't heard a word since the first telegram over a week ago. It was sent from Coalville, Utah. The trains weren't running because of a rockslide on west of there, so she was riding Badger cross-country. There is no way it should be a week before she reached another telegraph office. There's a train sitting in Rawlins waiting for the all-clear to continue west…been sitting there since the accident on up the track last week, according to the agent there. I'm going to Rawlins and catch that train to Coalville and start to backtrack the route that I would have taken if I were in her shoes and see if I can find her."

Marc had straightened in his chair as he realized the nature of Tall's visit to Medicine Bow. Marc and his wife, Linda, had two daughters who were lifelong best friends with Alaina. The two men were father to all three in a sense. They considered one another's children to be like their own and would give their lives, if necessary, to protect them.

The smile disappeared as Marc responded. "When are we leaving for Rawlins, tonight or in the morning?" he questioned.

"Do you feel like a long night in the saddle?" Tall came back.

"Sure enough! Been loafing most of the day, anyway. I'll go to the mercantile and gather up a few supplies while you grab a bite."

"Sounds like a plan. We can sleep on the train. We'll have to get a box car for the horses. I've got coffee so don't bother about that," Tall rambled on.

Marc hurried out the door as a young woman approached the table to receive his order. He suddenly realized he hadn't eaten all day."

What's on the stove back there?" he asked the waitress.

"Cook made a big pot of beef stew when he saw that storm coming," she offered. "Looks pretty good, too."

"That will be fine. Do you have any cornbread to go along with it?" he queried.

"Sure thing!" she returned as she scurried away.

* * *

The long journey from Medicine Bow to Rawlins was a challenging one even in daylight hours and good weather. But the storm clouds that had moved in earlier brought a steady downfall of powder, making the trail more difficult to recognize, and there were constant hills and gullies to maneuver. Under normal circumstances, Tall and Marc would have been able to take a train from Medicine Bow, but the schedule had been completely shut down when the tracks out west became impassable.

The gold, pocket watch from Tall's vest pocket indicated that it was three in the morning when they reached Walcott Junction and headed west toward Rawlins with still twenty miles to cover. The train wasn't scheduled to leave until noon, and there would be ample time to travel twenty miles were it not for the snow and the wind. Drifts had accumulated at every ridge and every gulley, sometimes measuring chest-deep on the horses. Pushing through them took time as well as energy that wasn't there to spare.

By mid-morning, both men began to worry. If they were to miss that train, there wouldn't be another one coming through for three days. They pushed their mounts to the limits. Both horses were lathered from perspiration even in the snow and cold north wind when the buildings of Rawlins came into view. Tall checked his watch again and breathed a sigh of relief when he realized it was nearing eleven o'clock. They would be pushing it to get there and arrange for a hookup to a box car for the horses before twelve.

The weary travelers were still a mile from town when the train whistle sounded.

"No!" Tall shouted. "They aren't supposed to leave until noon."

Without voicing a response, Marc touched Hermes with his spurs, and the big black gelding lunged ahead. The road was fairly snow-packed from constant use throughout the morning, and the big gelding seemed determined to live up to his name as he stretched out into long strides that covered the ground quickly.

The whistle sang out again as the engine built up steam, making ready to attempt breaking the cold, hard steel wheels loose from where they had remained for almost a week. The first few attempts were unsuccessful, but gradually the cars began to inch forward as the driver wheels on the engine spun round and round with a vengeance. Marc and Hermes never slowed, but sped right past the station and quickly intercepted the engineer. Marc waved his arms wildly and then pulled his slicker open revealing his badge. Immediately the train began to brake and soon came to a stop.

By the time Tall arrived, Marc had explained the situation to the engineer, and when he learned they were looking for one of the passengers that had been on the train that went into the river, he was more than happy to assist. He backed the train back into the yard to hook to a car for the horses while Tall checked with the telegraph agent for any messages, either from Alaina or from Jens. There was no word from either, so he and Marc loaded the horses and boarded the Pullman coach.

* * *

Two days later, the little train chugged up the last hill and alongside the station at Coalville, Utah. Marc and Tall went directly to the stock car and unloaded the horses. The sun had touched the treetops on the mountain to the west of town, so they led them directly to the livery stable and got them settled in with grain and plenty of hay for the night.

Before any thought for themselves, they went to check with the station master to see if he knew anything regarding Alaina's whereabouts. The train was pulling away and had just cleared the landing when they climbed the steps and entered the depot. The little man inside the ticket booth noticed the sheriff's badge immediately and met them at the window.

"May I be of assistance to you gentlemen?" he asked obligingly.

"Perhaps," Marc began.

Tall thought it best to allow Marc to do the questioning, thinking that Marc's badge would probably carry more weight than him being Alaina's father.

"We are here looking for a young girl who was on the train that went off into the river last week." Both men noticed the immediate change in the man's countenance.

"I'm sorry to inform you, sir," he began, while lowering his eyes toward the floor. "As of yet, we have been unable to locate any survivors from that terrible tragedy."

"No, you don't understand," Marc continued. "We are looking for a young girl who sent a wire gram to her father here," pointing toward Tall, "from this telegraph office a few days after the accident."

The man's face lit up as he looked up at them again. "Yes, I certainly remember that poor girl!" he expressed excitedly. "So, you are her father?" he asked as he directed his gaze at Tall.

"Yes, I'm her father," Tall conceded. "I received the telegram the very day it was sent from this office, but as of yet, have had no further word from her. Did she give you any indication as to her plans or particularly to her route of travel when she left here?"

"No, sir," the small man stated as a worried look crept into his eyes. "It was kinda strange the way she just left town without a word to anyone. I directed her to the livery and the boarding house down the street. She climbed up on that magnificent stallion of hers and rode off in that direction, and I never saw her again. I just assumed she left early the next morning."

"Is there any kind of law officer in town?" Tall inquired.

"Well, now, that's another peculiar thing," the agent volunteered. "We had a sheriff. Well, we had a man wearing a badge. In fact, your girl mentioned that the sheriff had questioned her as soon as she hit town, and she hadn't been completely honest with him. Gave her the heebie-jeebies, she said. He mistook her for a young man and wanted to know her business here.

"It was snowing right down when she arrived in town and had been most of the day. She was wearing two heavy coats and had her Stetson pulled down over her face with her hair stuffed up underneath." The agent made gestures with his hands as he tried to describe the scene to them. "No wonder he mistook her! I surely didn't recognize she was a girl until she took that hat off and shucked that slicker," the man chuckled.

"What's so peculiar, though, is a few days after your girl was here, the sheriff left town along with the mayor. Rode out heading east along the railroad, and no one in town has seen them since. Come to find out, the man wearing the star and claiming to be John Bascom from over around Provo is an imposter. Sheriff John Bascom was found dead. His body had been dumped into a deep ravine, and all of his personals, including his badge, were missing.

"When we got that bit of news, we began to question the disappearance of the foreman of the mine and a couple of young Mexicans that used to work up there keeping the place tidied up. All three of them disappeared at about that same time. The mayor told everyone that the mine foreman had received a letter from back east about an urgent family matter and that the young Mexicans just up and quit and went back to south Colorado where they came from."

Marc and Tall had listened intently to the man's story with growing concern. Had Alaina somehow gotten caught up in some mischief that the mayor and his murdering sidekick were involved with? Tall and Marc both knew her well. She had a knack for allowing her curiosity to overcome her better judgment.

They paid the livery man another visit before going to the boarding house. After describing Alaina and her stallion to him, he remembered her and informed them that she had indeed stabled the horse there but that she was gone before daylight the following morning when he came to open up.

Moving on to the boarding house, they acquired a room with two cots then described Alaina to the house attendant, questioning if she had stayed the night there. They received the same story the livery man had given them. Yes, she had stayed there, but was gone before breakfast.

* * *

After enjoying a good home-cooked meal, Marc and Tall retired to their room. Discussion revolved around the strange disappearance of the mayor and so-called sheriff, as well as the mine superintendent and two young Mexicans. Their thoughts then turned to Alaina and the possibility of how all of that might be connected with her leaving town during the night without anyone knowing.

After breakfast the next morning, the two men decided to split up and question everyone they could find about the mayor and the imposter sheriff, as well as the two Mexican workers and Alaina. They would meet back at the boarding house kitchen at high noon to compare notes and decide what their next course of action would be. Marc would contact members of the town council while Tall concentrated on business owners and folks on the street.

When Tall returned to the boarding house, Marc was already seated at the table where a small feast had been prepared and set. They agreed to save their conversation until it could be conducted in private but agreed that they needed to be traveling. They ate in silence, excused themselves and hurried to the livery and their horses.

After preparations were made for a long ride across-country, they headed east out of town, allowing the horses to pick their own leisurely gait while they talked. A new wall of clouds had erupted suddenly from the mountains above the little town and immediately began to cover the ground with a blanket of new snow.

Tall opened the conversation. "There's something really fishy going on here. The mine was going full steam, producing quality copper ore. People in town were working, the businesses were flourishing, and then, all of a sudden, everything collapsed and no one knows why. Although about everyone in town is convinced that the mayor and his friend, who was posing as a sheriff, had something to do with it. They were the only two in town who seemed to not be ruined by the sudden downturn of the town's economics."

"That's pretty much the same story I got," responded Marc. "The acting mayor told me that the town council had nothing to do with hiring that sheriff. The mayor just appointed him out of nowhere, and no one in town liked him, either. As far as Alaina goes though, I couldn't find out anything. Not a soul that I talked to ever knew she came to town."

"Same here," Tall agreed. "Which makes me think she just used good judgment, and intended it to be that way? If she was uncomfortable about the sheriff, the logical thing for her would be to stay out of his way. I'm trying to put myself in her shoes. I have three hundred miles to travel as the eagle flies, or three fifty to four hundred if I follow the route of the railroad. I know what I would do, and I think she would, too. She isn't afraid of the wilderness, so I think she would head east and northeast cross-country, right toward that range of mountains over yonder."

"Well, what are we waiting for? Let's skedaddle."

With that, the two men nudged their well-rested mounts into a gentle canter. Side by side, they galloped across the broad expanse of high plains toward the blue silhouette of mountain peaks before them. The snow had continued falling lightly throughout the afternoon but blue sky had broken through as suddenly as the clouds had come, and the sun was hiding behind the treetops on the western horizon as they rode into a swift but shallow stream that ran along the foot of a sheer red cliff.

"Let's camp here under the cottonwoods," Tall suggested. "If you'll make a fire and set up camp, I'll check up and downstream and see if there is any sign of Alaina. Don't expect to find anything after this snow, but I've got to look just the same."

Tall returned to camp as darkness closed in around them. He unsaddled Sassy and hobbled her near Hermes, giving her a quick rubdown with a handful of dried grass straw he found in a sheltered area under the trees.

"No sign of any fresh tracks in the snow," he offered as he approached the campfire where Marc had seated himself on a half-rotten fallen log. "Come daylight we'll head on over the mountain. There has to be some sign of her somewhere. If it's out there, I'll find it."

As soon as dawn broke and the eastern sky afforded enough light to pick their way through the rocks and sagebrush, Tall looked the mountain over and decided on a route of travel. The snowpack wasn't too bad as of yet, and so they intentionally crisscrossed the mountain ridges looking for any fresh tracks on the windswept slopes.

Four days later, they rode into a long valley on the north slope of the Uinta Mountains, tired and hungry for something other than jerky and ready for a warm bed instead of a thin bedroll spread out on a frozen, snow-covered ground. The two men had ridden in silence for most of the morning, working different directions, looking for tracks that would indicate Alaina had been through that way.

As they finally came near enough, Marc called out to Tall, "According to my calculations, we are in the general vicinity of Brown's Hole. I think it best that I go incognito for a while." He reached inside his slicker and removed the tin star from his vest and placed it in his vest pocket. Brown's Hole was the location of an old fort some fifty or sixty years back, but after abandonment by the military, it had become a favorite hideout for several notorious outlaws.

"I don't know if it is still as rough as the last time I was here, but we need to be careful," he added. "If there has been a young girl through this country, though, someone in that bunch that hangs out there would know about it."

"Well then, I want to go there and find out," Tall stated emphatically.

After scouting around for the better part of the afternoon, the two travelers rode into a cluster of ramshackle log structures situated along a small spring-fed stream. Several horses were tied to a rickety hitch rail in front of one of the larger of the buildings. They stepped down and draped their reins over the rail, looking around suspiciously to see if anyone had observed their arrival. Seeing no one, they moved to the door of the most stable looking of the buildings, and that appeared to be the main attraction in this out-of-the-way nest of ne're-do-wells.

The stuffy, smoke-filled room was crowded with a dozen or more rough looking men and three middle-aged women. The women were clad in low-cut costume dresses like one might expect to see in a Denver saloon but certainly not in a rundown, shack-of-a-barroom such as this. None of the three were particularly attractive, even with all the face paint they wore. One of the women moved toward them as they walked toward the bar along the back wall.

"Good evening, gentlemen," she began. "I'm Ann Bassett, and the two ladies behind you, who incidentally have their hands on your six shooters at this very moment, are my sister, Josie, and my friend, Marge."

It was a slick move. The two men realized too late they had been set up. They felt the pistols being lifted from their holsters and watched as every man in the room turned their attention toward them with guns drawn, as well.

One of the men took the lead and voiced the question for the group. "Now that the ladies have introduced themselves, suppose you two do likewise. Who are you, and what business do you have in our little neck o' the woods?"

All the while the man spoke, each of the intruders felt the cold steel of their own revolvers pressing between their shoulder blades. They had considered the risk before riding in, but both had agreed it was worth it to get the information they so direly needed. The woman who had introduced herself as Ann moved in close and began going through their pockets, first the slickers and then their vests.

"Well, well, look what we have here," she squawked, as she raised Marc's badge into the air for all in the room to see. Neither Marc nor Tall had counted on this.

"You two have got a lot of nerve, I'll give ye that," the spokesman of the bunch continued. "We don't much like lawmen around here. We ain't hung no lawman in quite some time, neither. Used to be a pretty common occurrence, but most of 'um wised up and made it their business to stir clear of Brown's Hole."

"Gentlemen, let's not be too hasty, now," a voice echoed from the far edge of the room. "The one with the badge is none other than Marcus Augustus Frost, namesake of one Marcus Aurelius Antonius Augustus, great emperor of Rome."

Both Tall and Marc recognized the voice right away, and they each breathed a soft sigh of relief to find that they had at least one friend in the room.

Butch Cassidy pushed through the crowd as he went on. "This other fellow is the one man who came close to setting me on the straight and narrow. This here is Tall Johnson." Butch reached out his hand as he spoke, and Tall gladly took it. "You men can put your guns away. I don't have even an inkling of an idea what brings these two to our doorstep on this cold wintery night, but I am most certain they aren't here looking for any of you. You ladies can give the irons back."

Everyone in the room complied without so much as a moment's hesitation. Butch motioned for them to join him at a table in the corner. Another man who looked to be about the same age as Butch and Marc was already seated with his back to the wall.

"Sundance, I think you have met Marc, but I want to make you acquainted with Tall Johnson," Butch said as he nodded toward Tall.

"My pleasure, I'm sure," the man expressed, as he leaned forward across the table, extending his hand to shake. Tall accepted the invitation and gave him a long steady grip as he looked directly into his eyes.

"Pleasure is all mine," Tall responded. "Believe I've heard your name a time or two. You know how talk goes around. Figure some of its true, and some, probably not. At any rate, I've never been one to judge another man. I figure that ought to be left to someone who knows all the facts.

"Now, to get to the real reason we are here. Butch, you know my daughter, Alaina. Well, you haven't seen her for several years, and she's not the little tot she used to be. Marc and I are trying to locate her. She left Coalville, Utah, a few weeks ago headed cross-country for home. When I didn't hear from her, Marc and I rode a rail car to Coalville thinking we might find her trail and determine why she hadn't made it home yet. Marc figured if she came through this country one of you gents would know about it."

Butch stood from his chair and let out a shrill whistle. The room grew suddenly silent while he explained the situation and asked if anyone had seen or heard of a young girl traveling alone through the valley. No one spoke up.

The four men passed the rest of the evening in conversation…some about old times on the stage line when Marc and Butch drove for Tall, some about Butch and Sundance and the stories that were being told about their adventures involving train robberies and Wells Fargo gold shipments. Finally, they spoke about Coalville and the strange disappearance of the mayor and imposter sheriff.

Butch lowered his voice as he responded to the remarks about Coalville. He leaned in toward the center of the table as he spoke, "Word is, there is something going on in Encampment, Wyoming—something to do with the smelter plant there. The two men you're referring to came through here a few days ago looking for a couple of back-up men with experience for some kind of heist they've got planned for early spring. They wouldn't give any details, of course, but said they would be back in a few months.

"Just be careful if you run into these hombres. They are bad medicine, especially the one who passed himself off as a sheriff. He will kill a man and not blink twice. They left here saying they were headed for Green River." With that, Butch rose from his chair and motioned for the other three to follow. "Let's get out of here. Sundance and I have a shack we laid claim too. We can get some rest there, and you won't have to worry about anyone bothering you."

Marc and Tall first went to their horses and pulled their gear off, saddle and bridle, to allow them freedom to move around. Toting the rigs over their shoulders, they followed the other two men inside. They dozed restlessly through the night, and as soon as daylight came, they were glad to be back on their way. They talked over the possibility that Alaina could have followed the train route back through Utah and Wyoming and decided to angle northeastward toward Green River and Rock Springs.

6. Wrestling with Mother Nature

Weeks became months. Winter descended upon Alaina's little world with a fury. Alaina had to spend much of her time making sure Badger was provided with enough grazing, however unsavory it might be, to keep him going. She had depleted the grain in her saddle bags long ago and observed the slow reduction in his body weight but knew that it was normal for range animals wintering in the northwestern mountainous country. He would quickly regain the weight when the nutritious green grass returned in the spring.

Another major concern for her was gathering enough firewood to warm the spacious cave. The inclement weather outside did keep Alaina and the girl in close quarters, however, and her continued recovery provided more and more opportunity for the two of them to attempt to communicate.

With serious effort from each of them, they had worked out a system to get their point across to one other. Broken English, broken Spanish, and sometimes very peculiar sign language, all intermixed, served them fairly well. The very first concern for Alaina was to learn the girl's name.

After many attempts of pointing to herself and repeating her name, "Alaina," the faintest smile appeared on the girl's lips, and she said, "*Anarosa, mi nombre es Anarosa, Anarosa Torres.*"

"*Anarosa*," mused Alaina, "Ann Rose, what a beautiful name for a beautiful young Mexican lady."

The bruising and swelling had all finally gone from the small, dainty face of olive complexion. The cuts had healed nicely with only the slightest trace of scaring that Alaina felt confident would eventually become unnoticeable. The swelling in her arms and leg had proven to be from fractures rather than breaks, leaving no permanent disfigurement.

Alaina frequently thought back to the bloody, beaten, broken heap she had discovered on the sandbar of the little mountain stream not so long ago and wondered what kind of person could have done such a thing to the sweet, attractive young girl who sat before her. The answer to that, she would not be long finding out.

"Ann Rose," Alaina began, "I need to take you to Coalville as soon as you can ride."

With a wild flurry of hands and an avalanche of Spanish, hardly any of which Alaina understood—other than the emphatic repeat of "*No!*" Anarosa frantically objected to the proposal. Her objection continued for several minutes with fear creasing her forehead and tears streaming down her pretty cheeks as she began to move toward the opening of the cave.

Alaina stepped between her and the doorway, holding up her hands in front of her. "Wait, wait, Anarosa, calm down. Hold on a minute," she pleaded, as she motioned her back to her perch on the small boulder she had been seated on.

"What's wrong?" Slowly and thoughtfully Alaina tried to translate the question into Spanish. "*Lo queue está mal?*"

Another avalanche of Spanish issued forth with hands waving excitedly in the air. Again, Alaina held her hands up, as if to say, *Slow down!*

Anarosa moved to the little pile of smaller sticks that Alaina had gathered for kindling for the fire. Choosing one of the smallest, she knelt to the dirt floor of the cave and began to draw something. Alaina immediately recognized the shape of a star. Anarosa pointed to the crude image in the dirt and blurted, "Coalville, *policia*," and then pointed toward the wounds all over her body. "Coalville *policia*, to me."

Alaina stumbled backward, her face turning ashen white. She understood fully what Anarosa was trying desperately to tell her, as well as why she would be so terrified at the mere mention of the town. The little bit of information that Alaina had acquired about him in the few hours she had spent there convinced her that the sheriff of Coalville would be capable of hurting people, even unmercifully.

"Okay, okay, *bueno*," she insisted soothingly. "We won't go, *no vamos*." A definite expression of relief came over Anarosa's entire body.

* * *

The following weeks passed with no change in the weather. There continued to be a seemingly endless cycle of snowstorms followed by warm sunny days of snow melt. During the stormy days, the two girls worked on their communicative skills with one another. Each of them proved to be good students, quick to learn the others dialect, and soon they talked about everything.

Over time, Anarosa related to Alaina how she and her brother Miguel had been employed at the copper mine in Coalville. Their duties were mostly custodial, she cleaning the offices and meeting rooms, and he keeping the grounds and doing light maintenance chores. The mayor of Coalville had been one of the more familiar faces around the mine, and then after the sheriff came to town, the two of them and the manager at the mine became noticeable companions.

One-night Miguel had agreed to help her with a complete, extensive scouring of the entire office complex. The undertaking had carried them near to midnight, and as they were putting finishing touches on the storeroom, a group of men entered the office unaware of their presence and began a discussion that eventually became a heated argument interrupted by the sudden report of a handgun.

The sheriff had pulled his revolver and killed the manager of the mine. Miguel was much better with English than Anarosa and had understood quite enough to realize that the argument had been over a scheme that the mayor and sheriff were proposing. It was their intent to intercept a large amount of money that was to be transferred at some time in the coming year to a copper mine and smelter plant in Southern Wyoming.

The discussion had revealed that they had been successful in doing the very thing at Coalville with no one being the wiser, and since they had no obvious connection to the smelter plant in Wyoming, the job would be even less risky for them. The manager of the mine had battled with his own conscience since they had pulled off the Coalville heist. He became very vocally opposed to the plan for the Wyoming mine and threatened to expose them if they insisted on going through with it.

Miguel and Anarosa had remained silently cowering in the corner of the storeroom and would have gone undetected had the sheriff not decided to conceal the dead body of the mine superintendent until he could return with a buckboard to transport it into the hills.

The discovery of the two hidden witnesses complicated matters tremendously. They had not only heard about the crimes already committed and the plans to duplicate the scheme elsewhere, but they had also witnessed the murder of the manager of the mine. The sheriff had immediately pulled his revolver and held them at gun point while the mayor tied and gagged them.

Laboriously, Anarosa had described what then happened to herself and her brother. The sheriff had returned with a buckboard, loaded them, along with the dead man, into the shallow bed of the wagon and hauled them far into the hills where he proceeded to attempt to beat them to death, first with his fists, then his pistol, and finally with the butt of his riffle. Eventually, Anarosa had regained consciousness, and after discovering her brother was dead, crawled and dragged herself to the edge of the stream where Alaina had found her.

Alaina had listened with astonishment and much growing interest to Anarosa's narrative of her and Miguel's tragic encounter with the sheriff of Coalville, understanding completely her horror of returning there. There was the other matter though, that set her head to reeling, the scheme about a copper mine and smelter plant in Southern Wyoming. The only such operation she was familiar with was at Encampment, Wyoming. Her mother had been involved with a court case involving the burning of the smelter plant there a few years previously.

Then recently, every newspaper in the state had reported another fire. There was talk of the possibility of foul play, although there was some evidence that it had been the result of some fault in the wiring in the new electric system that had just been installed. Electricity had been made available there by the installation of a hydro-electric generator on the giant wooden flume that channeled water from the North Fork of the Encampment River down the mountain to the smelter plant. Encampment was the first town in Wyoming to be able to enjoy the new luxury of electric lights. Some had claimed they were the first town west of the

Mississippi. Alaina had been there with her Dad and had actually seen the modern wonder.

This news of new investment money coming in from the east must mean that plans were in motion to rebuild the plant, or to make new improvements, or both. Whatever the case, she was now confronted with another dilemma, how to get the two of them to Encampment ahead of that imposter sheriff and ex-mayor of Coalville. Trying to catch an eastbound train would place Anarosa in grave danger if they were discovered, but it would be two or three more months before most of the snow was gone in the mountains.

They could not hope to maneuver through the two hundred miles or more of rough terrain that lay ahead on one horse. Even if the hope were there, Alaina didn't think Badger would ever tolerate a second passenger.

Anarosa quietly watched the worrisome expressions and deep concentration play across her friend's face. Curious of the reasons, she finally broke the silence. "*Lo que le molesta,*" she inquired. "What is wrong?"

Alaina was startled by the sound of her voice. She had been so deep in her own thoughts that she had become completely unaware of Anarosa's presence. She thought for a moment, not sure how to relate their predicament.

"*Necesitamos otro caballo,*" Alaina emphasized each word carefully, unsure of herself. "We need another horse."

Ann Rose smiled and nodded. "*Sí, en el valle,*" she responded. "*Caballo,* in valley, run free."

It was Alaina's turn to smile now. Yes, she had seen the mustangs in the valley as she hunted for game. "I have no lariat, *no lazo,*" she explained.

"No, you need *no lazo,*" Ann Rose insisted. "I show you."

Anarosa carefully explained to Alaina how she could capture one of the mustangs by riding in close on Badger, and how, after running side by side for a distance, she could leap from Badger onto the other horse. She described in detail what she could expect from the other horse.

If she could coax Badger to continue to run along beside it, the mustang would run until it became weary and Alaina would be able to loop the lower jaw with a war bridle of a sort. Then before the horse came to a stop, she could have it obeying the rein.

Alaina listened with mixed emotion until Ann Rose was silent. "You have seen someone do this?" she quizzed.

"I have done this," Anarosa responded, "Many times. Miguel and me...we would capture and sell the mustang pony to buy food. I can show you everything."

For the next several days, they talked about this new venture. Alaina could see how it might be possible. She had stood in the saddle many times with Badger in a slow canter across a flat plain but never in a flat out run. And leaping from one horse to another in full flight could be risky, to say the least. Still, Anarosa assured her that she had accomplished the feat on many occasions.

Well, if she can do it, I can, she finally told herself. After all, hadn't she practically lived on the back of a horse her whole life?

She quizzed Ann Rose over and over about every detail of the entire venture, from how long to run beside the other horse before the leap, to how to go about exercising a clean leap without becoming entangled or falling off of the other horse, to how to place the war bridle over the lower jaw of the new mount. She asked about how soon to begin coaxing the mustang to respond to the bridle and how long to continue riding before dismounting and what would happen when she did dismount. How would they ever catch the pony again?

Anarosa explained that they needed to build a small corral among the pines near the cave and that she should ride the mustang into the corral before dismounting. From there, Alaina could leave the rest to her. She would gentle the pony, and within a few days, they could be on their way.

7. The Capture

Work on the small corral progressed rapidly. Alaina scoured the surrounding hills for stands of lodge pole pines and particularly any that had been pushed down in previous years by snow slides. These small, dead logs she dragged back to a place they had chosen near the cave. The chore would have been much easier with the use of a lariat.

She was pretty upset with herself for not leaving her rope on her saddle while preparing for the trip to San Francisco. Her thoughts were to only take what she felt she would absolutely need, and a lariat just did not seem to fit in her list of 'Articles I Will Need in the City.' Now, however, a lariat rope would tremendously simplify the difficult task of capturing a wild mustang.

Mark that down to experience, she thought to herself. *Next time you leave home, take everything you own because whatever you leave behind will be the one thing you need the most.*

Rose, that's how Alaina had decided to address Anarosa, and she seemed to like the shortened version. Rose had given her instructions on preparing for the leap from Badger to the mustang. Alaina had made a war bridle and lead rope out of rawhide from a deer skin she had stretched when they first arrived at the cave. It had cured out nicely, and after Rose became able to use her arms, she had scraped the flesh from the one side and hair from the other using Alaina's knife.

The knife was another of the questionable articles she had argued with herself about while packing for the trip. It was a long war knife that had been given to her father by his Indian captor when he was a child. It was an heirloom of a sort, as well as an extremely useful tool in the outdoors.

Alaina was glad of her choice to bring it. Life during the past few months would have been much more challenging without its many uses. She would have to remember to thank her dad again for trusting her with such a prized possession.

Preparations were finally complete, and Alaina felt that she was ready for the big day. She saddled Badger just as dawn was breaking in the arroyo. She had stripped everything off of her saddle that might cause her to become entangled when she made the leap to the other horse. The only item remaining was the small canteen. Saddlebag, rifle scabbard, and latigo strings that held her bed roll in place were all removed and left at the cave.

She made inventory of the necessary items for the capture. The war bridle to place around the lower jaw of the mustang was tucked into her waistband, and the lead rope was attached to Badger's bridle. She would hold on to that when she transferred from him to the pony to assure Badger would continue to run along beside them. She carried a small pouch filled with jerky in her pocket in case she was away longer than planned.

Alaina felt a twinge of nervous excitement as she began the short ride to the valley below. She had practiced with Badger a little each day while they were preparing the corral. She felt completely at ease about perching on her feet in the saddle at full gallop, but everything from there on would be completely left to chance. She had no way to prepare herself for that leap that had to be executed without a hitch or she would find herself rolling through cactus and sagebrush practically at the speed of a locomotive. She dreaded to think what she would look like were that to happen.

Concentration, she kept reminding herself. *Concentrate, concentrate, concentrate.*

Having explored the hills for miles around since they came to the cave, Alaina knew the favorite pools where the mustang herds came to water. She had risen early in order to be waiting in the brush when they showed up for their early morning drink. She had hardly gotten settled when a small band of mustang ponies proved her expectations to be correct.

Her heart pounded furiously in anticipation as she inspected each horse in the herd. She had already concluded that the pony of choice would need to be one that was large enough and strong enough to carry a rider up and down mountains, possibly through belly-deep snow drifts for hours at a time.

She took close inventory and made her move. The instant Badger moved toward them, the mustang ponies lifted their heads from the water. They realized the human presence and their danger and wheeled and bolted through the sagebrush that lined the bank of the pool. Alaina called for and was rewarded with every ounce of strength from the rippling muscles of the stallion beneath her. They were upon the stampeding herd of ponies in mere seconds.

The one Alaina had chosen was in the lead, proving her assessment of his being superior to all the rest. She gave Badger another nudge with her heels and sucked air through her lips, making a squeaking sound. He shot forward with renewed determination, covering the distance between himself and the leader in only a few long strides. Alaina found herself looking down on the back of the mustang pony, trying to recall every detail Rose had told her about how long to wait before making that leap of faith.

The mustang stallion had swerved away from the rest of the herd, circling to the right. Alaina was just gathering her nerve to lift her feet to make ready for the leap when the paint pony suddenly reached back toward Badger, attempting to nip him on the shoulder. Badger avoided the aggression by veering slightly to the left. Seeing his advance had caused Badger's slight retreat, the mustang turned toward him and attacked.

Badger accommodated his challenge by charging into him with the full force of his body. Alaina realized what was about to happen and grabbed the saddle horn and held on for dear life. The two animals clashed together and immediately squared off for a battle for dominance, ignoring completely the presence of a third party still astride the larger of the two.

This was not at all a part of the plan! Alaina realized her dire mistake in choosing another stallion. What was she thinking anyway? Right now, she needed to act fast. One blow from one of the steel-like hooves of the Mustang stallion would break an arm or leg, and a blow to her head could kill her.

Badger had never failed to obey her wishes, no matter what might be at stake. She hoped he would not let her down now. She pulled backward on the reins with all of her strength, yelling, "Back…back…*back!*" To her relief, he began to back away.

The mustang stallion reared, pawing the air with his front feet and piercing the crisp morning air with a bone-chilling squeal, but he made no advance toward the intruders. He then bolted and circled around them, galloping full speed back toward the herd.

Alaina sat motionless in the saddle for a moment, her body trembling from the unexpected near catastrophe. After recovering her composure, she pulled Badger around and rode back to the cave.

Rose was waiting in the doorway, and seeing Alaina returning astride Badger, she came to meet her. Alaina told her all about her thrilling experience with no detail omitted, even the part about her almost soiling her saddle. She and Rose talked and laughed for hours about their first unsuccessful attempt while making plans for tomorrow. The morning was clear and warm with no sign of a change of weather, so they set about with their daily routine around the camp, each one eagerly anticipating what tomorrow might bring.

Dawn the following morning found Alaina and Badger concealed within a thicket of pussy willows upwind of another pool that showed, by both old and fresh hoof prints, to be an active watering hole for numerous mustangs. She chewed on a piece of fresh venison jerky as she looked over the first small band that came to drink. They were all small in height and scrawny looking in body weight. Alaina thought they were probably bachelor stallions that had banded together for the winter, having been driven from their prospective herds by the dominant stallion.

She had determined to be more selective in her choice of a candidate for a companion saddle horse this time. She watched another band of ponies come and go, wondering if the experience yesterday might have dulled her nerve. Was she really being selective or stalling out of fear? She had never been whipped by anything before and was determined she would not allow it to happen now.

She snapped back from her woolgathering, that's what her dad called daydreaming, at the appearance of a large band of ponies moving in from an arroyo across the stream from her vantage point. Immediately her gaze went to a large bay horse. She watched as they were hazed along by a black stallion. That settled her first and main question. The bay was not the dominate stallion, which meant it was more than likely a mare. Otherwise the black would not allow it near the herd.

Alaina took note of the war bridle in her waistband and the lead rope that was wrapped around the saddle horn and prepared to make her move. She waited until every head had lowered to drink and then charged from the thicket straight for the bay. She had covered half the distance before the large bay mare realized what was happening.

The mare whirled and fell in behind the others who had scrambled away immediately upon Alaina and Badger's emerging from the willows. However, she quickly made up the loss of time by moving up near the front of the herd. Alaina mimicked the earlier attempt, asking Badger for every ounce of strength, receiving his response with him charging through the herd alongside the bay.

Alaina pressed closer against the big mare, forcing her away from the other horses. Looking in the direction of travel, Alaina saw no obstacle that might cause the bay to dodge or slow unexpectedly, so she prepared to make her move. Unwrapping the lead rope from the horn of the saddle, she took one turn around her hand to prevent losing it, yet not becoming attached hard and fast in case something went awry.

She lifted her feet into the seat of the saddle and took a deep breath. Alaina made a conscious survey of the back of the adjacent animal and sprang across the distance, landing firmly astride the large bay mare, burying both hands in the long flowing mane of the bay. Badger continued to hold his position just as she had hoped.

To her pleasant surprise, the mare made no attempt to unseat her, nor did she show any evidence of tiring or slowing. Alaina held on tightly with her left hand while she slipped the war bridle from her waistband with her right. Then leaning forward, keeping rhythm with the speeding animal, she reached out with the loop of the stiff rawhide rein and slipped it over the mare's lower jaw. She pulled back gently to fasten it securely in place behind the mare's teeth, and to her astonishment the bay slowed down the instant she pulled back.

Shocked by this seeming response, she decided to try it again. She pulled back again, simultaneously uttering the command, "Whoa!"

The big mare came to a complete stop so quickly Alaina was almost thrown from her back and jerked away by the lead rope attached to Badger's bridle. After managing to regain her balance, she nudged the bay with her heels, clucking to her simultaneously.

The mare responded by moving forward. Alaina then pulled her to the right with immediate response, then to the left with like response. A broad smile lit up Alaina's girlish face as she realized the big bay mare was a well-trained mount that had either been allowed to run free or had been recruited by the black stallion from the remuda of some cattleman in the area.

Badger had approached them slowly, prancing and squealing as he reached to sniff at the muzzle of the big mare. Alaina leaned toward him and removed the lead rope from his bridle. She quickly fashioned a loop and slipped it over the mare's head and slid to the ground. She gave her a gentle rub between the ears and down the front of her nose, to which the bay responded by sniffing her face and then her hair. Alaina giggled to herself as she stepped into the stirrup and pointed Badger back toward camp with the mare in tow.

When Rose spied Alaina coming toward the cave riding Badger and leading the mare, she came running to meet her. Alaina stepped from the saddle and handed her the lead rope. "Here is your mount," she stated as she chuckled.

Rose stood speechless while Alaina walked around the animal, scrutinizing every inch of her body for any sign of a brand. The discovery that there was none relieved her considerably. The last thing she needed was for someone to recognize the mare as their own and accuse them of horse theft. They had enough to deal with already.

Out of curiosity, Alaina removed her saddle from Badger and placed it on the mare. She stood without even a flinch while Alaina pulled the front cinch strap tight and fastened the back cinch loosely underneath her belly. Alaina then removed Badger's bridle, slipped it over the mare's head and stepped into the saddle. She put her through a quick reining workout around the small clearing then pulled her to a stop and dismounted.

"After all of that work and stress," she began, "I could have ridden up to her and dropped the lead rope over her head and led her back to camp." They both laughed at the prospect. "We spent days building a corral we don't even need."

The two girls busied themselves for the rest of the day preparing to begin their long journey toward Encampment, Wyoming, and the smelter plant located there. Alaina had given considerable thought as to whether they should even bother. She realized that to go there would be placing herself and Rose into harm's way.

When she brought the subject up to Rose, however, Rose refused to even entertain the thought of not going. She wanted desperately to see that the fake sheriff and ex-mayor of Coalville were not only stopped from their dastardly scheme but made to pay for the death of her brother, Miguel. She figured the manager of the mine at Coalville got what was coming to him, but neither she, nor Miguel, deserved what they got. Rose knew she would die, if necessary, to see that her brother's death was avenged and justice was served.

With that, Alaina considered the question settled, for it was not a matter of choice for her. She was bound by conscience to do the right thing, no matter what. The right thing here was certain. They must try to reach Encampment before the crime was committed, and if possible, bring the lawbreakers to justice.

Before dawn the following morning, the two girls had broken camp, packing everything away in saddle bags and the bedroll. They each stuffed their pockets with jerky they had been preparing for the past several weeks. There was also a large bundle wrapped in buckskin inside the bedroll in case fresh game wasn't available.

Alaina had sketched out a crude map in the dirt floor of the cave the evening before, explaining to Rose their approximate location, the different mountain ranges that lay ahead and where Encampment was located in relation to it all. As daylight began filtering into the little arroyo, Alaina gave Rose a boost astride the bay mare before swinging up onto Badger and led the way back down into the canyon below.

They followed the canyon back to where Alaina had first ridden upon the stream and discovered Rose lying unconscious on the sandbar. Alaina quickly took note of the eastern sky, made apparent by the approaching sunrise, took inventory of the mountain before them from one end to the other and chose a route that would take them northeastward.

She nudged Badger with her heels and led the way toward a gentle ridge that would take them up and over the first mountain that lay between them and Encampment, Wyoming…and whatever awaited them there.

8. The Long Road Home

Both Alaina and Rose were familiar with the outdoors and were aware of what to expect traveling across mountainous country in winter. Alaina, having been reared in the Wyoming high plains and mountains, was at home on horseback in deep snow. Both Badger and the bay were accustomed to the difficulty of pushing through snow drifts as well as carefully choosing their footing along treacherous game trails.

Alaina led them along the higher ridges when possible, well away from the edge of any sheer cliffs. When it became necessary to cross from one ridge to another, she would scour the country ahead with her binoculars to locate the gentler slopes by which to travel. When the horses tired, she would look for the best sheltered spot to make camp for the night.

They rode mostly in silence, giving their undivided attention to the trail. The first three days were difficult. Alaina calculated that they only accomplished around ten to twelve miles a day. The forth day brought them out onto a wide, open plain. Wind and sun had either melted the snow or piled it in small drifts beside the sage bushes and cactus.

"Do you feel like making up some time?" she quizzed Rose.

"*Si,*" she replied excitedly, "*Vamos!*"

Alaina gently nudged Badger with her heels. He seemed pleased to finally be able to stretch into an easy canter. The big bay mare moved along effortlessly beside him as they devoured the plain with their giant strides. Before sunset, they had entered the foothills of another mountain range. Alaina slowed Badger to a walk, allowing him and the mare to cool before stopping for the night.

Two fairly high mountains formed a saddle directly in front of them, so she headed for the saddle, hoping to find a sheltered campsite with enough grass left from the past summer to fill the horses. Also, she hoped to possibly find a snowshoe rabbit for a nice meal for herself and Rose. But when they topped out on the ridge, to their surprise, the valley below was covered with cattle.

A small river ran along the mountain on the other side of the valley. Nestled in a nook of the mountain was a log cabin surrounded by pens and outbuildings. Smoke spiraled from the chimney of the cabin, issuing a gentle invitation to the two young women. The thought of a good meal and sitting around a warm hearth sipping hot coffee was inviting indeed.

Could they be so fortunate? Alaina wondered, as she pulled up on the stallion to access the situation more thoroughly. *"¿Qué te parece.* What do you think?" Alaina quizzed Rosa.

"*Si,* let's go," she quickly replied, nodding toward the cabin with a smile from ear to ear.

They descended slowly into the secluded little homestead and reined their mounts toward the cabin. They stopped in the middle of the shallow river to allow the horses to drink liberally, and as they climbed up the gentle bank near the cabin, a tall slender man emerged from a small barn with a milk pail in his hand. He spied the riders approaching and stopped to wait for them to reach him before going on toward the house.

"Howdy there," he greeted as they drew near.

Each of the girls gestured a hello with a wave of the hand.

"Seldom get visitors way out here," he continued. "And never two young girls such as yerselves ridin' alone! Gettin' late and it's a fair piece to any settlement. Yer welcome to put yer horses up in the barn and come in fer some vittles. Wife'll have a bite fixed directly. Might not be what yer used ter, but it'll do to drive the chill outta yer bones."

"Thanks, Mister," Alaina returned. "We really would be obliged. We've been on the trail for quite some time. Real home-cooking sounds wonderful."

"Well, light on down an' make yer'selves to home. There's grain in the bin in there. Give them fine lookin' animals a double helpin', and fork 'em some hay down from the loft. I'll go ahead to the house an' let the woman know we got comp'ny."

Alaina and Rose located an empty stall inside the barn, pulled the saddles from the mounts, gave them each some grain and hay along with a good rub down and then made their way up to the cabin. The smell of hot biscuits set Alaina's mouth to watering as they tapped on the door. A somewhat attractive young woman appearing to be in her mid-twenties came to the door and extended a warm welcome to the two girls.

"I'm Martha Dodd, and this is my husband Frank," she said, motioning toward the table where the man was already seated. She had set out two extra plates on the small table in the corner. She motioned for them to be seated while she scurried back and forth between the wood cook stove and the table.

She filled glasses with milk and brought both biscuits and cornbread, along with a pot filled with pinto beans and a cast iron skillet full of fresh cooked gravy. She filled the last space left on the little table with a platter of fried venison steaks. Alaina and Rosa looked at one another, eyes wide with excitement, hardly believing their good fortune.

The hosts of the evening seemed to have compassion for their unexpected guests. They asked no questions nor spoke directly to the two girls until they had eaten their fill and sat back in their chairs with looks of satisfaction on their faces. They all remained around the table for a good long while just making small talk. The young couple seemed as eager for company as the two girls were for home comforts.

After a time, Frank excused himself, muttering something about toting in some wood and getting a fire goin'. The three ladies cleaned off the table and washed and dried the dishes while chatting away about the little homestead and about Alaina and Rose making such a trip this time of year. Alaina had told them they were headed to Encampment, Wyoming, but stopped short of stating the reason for their need to make the journey cross-country in wintertime.

After half an hour, Frank came back in and told Alaina and Rose that the bunkroom off of the barn would be nice and warm directly and that he had carried in enough wood to last through the night. The two showed their surprise and voiced their deep appreciation for the hospitality.

"You mentioned a settlement when we first rode in," Alaina began, "how far is it from here exactly?"

"Well, it ain't 'bout ten miles as the eagle flies, but it's a purdy hard day's ride, cuz o' tha lay o' tha land. Little place called Vernal," Frank answered.

Alaina wasn't familiar with that name. "Is it in Colorado?" she quizzed.

"Nope," Frank responded. "Utah. But not too fer from the Colorado line, and not too fer from the Wyomin' line neither."

"Is there a telegraph there?" Alaina questioned further.

"Nope, ye'll have ta go all the way to Steamboat Springs, er else go north to Green River to the railroad," Frank instructed.

"How far is it to Green River?" Alaina came back.

"'Bout a hundred-mile due north o' right there where you sit," Frank answered, smiling.

Alaina had no intention of going near the railroad, but with the one question, she had learned exactly where she was in relation to Encampment, Wyoming.

"So, Baggs, Wyoming, would be about a hundred miles northeast from here, then. Is that about right?" Alaina asked.

"That ud be 'bout right, I'm thinkin'," Frank replied. "You cud follow the Yampa from Vernal to where it joins up with the Little Snake. Iffin ye keep with the main fork o' tha Snake, it'll take ye right strait to Baggs."

Alaina and Rose were well spent by now. They thanked their hosts again and excused themselves for the night. They discovered that the bunkroom was indeed toasty warm. Two wooden bunks with corn shuck mattresses, a small table with one straight-backed chair, and what Alania's dad called a sheepherder's stove furnished the little room. Frank had left a pail of fresh water on the table beside a wash basin. A towel and wash cloth hung draped over the back of the chair.

Alaina made mention of the fact that Martha had probably placed them there in case of unexpected guests such as they. The two girls took turns washing up in the comfort of the warm bunkroom before bringing their blankets from the barn and turning in.

Alaina awakened to the crowing of a rooster somewhere out in the cattle pens. She looked across the room to see Rose rubbing her eyes and yawning sleepily. Neither one seemed in a hurry to get up, but a few minutes later, there was a gentle rap on the door, and Frank informed them that breakfast was ready.

They hurriedly washed up and raced to the little cabin where Martha had prepared eggs, biscuits, gravy, and another platter of fried venison steaks. Coffee perked on the wood stove, sending up a rich aroma for which, for months, Alaina had longed for. The girls were seating themselves when Frank came in informing them that he had taken the liberty to give the horses another double portion of grain, figuring that they had a long hard journey ahead of them and the extra steam would be good for 'em. Alaina thanked him and wanted to know how they could repay him for his kindness.

"Not necessary," he mumbled, as he sat down and began to dig into the fine meal.

When everyone was finished, the ladies once again worked together to clean off the table and wash the dishes, putting everything in its proper place. Alaina had one more cup of coffee before washing her cup. She and Rose gave Martha a hug and bid her goodbye, promising if they ever came near their place again, they would stop in for a visit.

Alaina saddled Badger, and as they led the horses from the barn, Frank came from one of the other outbuildings carrying an entire rig consisting of bridle, saddle, saddle blanket, and saddle bags.

"Got a proposition fer ye," he stated in a matter of fact tone. "I'd be willin' to len' you this here riggin', the bags are full o' grain, iffin ye wud promise to return fer a visit when ye git a chance. Don't have ta be soon, jist whenever ye can. The wife gits mighty lonely out here. We seldom git to the settlement, 'n' you two are the first to come by in more na year, I reckin. I don't need two rigs. Seldom go horseback, anyways."

Alaina looked quizzically toward Rose, who again was smiling from ear to ear and nodding affirmatively.

"I could pay you for it," Alaina volunteered.

"Well now, that there 'ud pretty much kill the whole plan," returned Frank. "I figure you're good fer yer word, so if ye say ye'll bring it back, I 'spect ye will."

The girls agreed that once their business was settled in Encampment they would make it their first priority to come for a return visit. They each shook Frank's hand to seal the deal with a gentleman's agreement and set in to putting the saddle and bridle on the mare.

* * *

Frank's statement that the journey over the mountain to Vernal was a hard day's ride was quite an understatement. Darkness had enveloped the basin within which the town was situated as they rode up to the hitching rail in front of the livery stable. Alaina had dug a small coin purse from her saddle bag before leaving the little ranch that morning and placed it in her coat pocket.

She had left for San Francisco well prepared to not run short of cash, and thus far had spent very little. She arranged for stalls for the horses and asked directions to a hotel. She and Rose stopped in the café downstairs for another good meal, then Alaina paid for a room, and they turned in early.

The morning was far spent when the girls decided they should get up. Neither of the two could recall the last time they had the luxury of sleeping on a real bed and remaining in it until feeling completely rested. They had discussed the matter the night before, and each agreed that a day out of the saddle would do both them and the horses a world of good and would probably not make any difference as for as the business ahead of them was concerned.

Their main worry was to get to Encampment before the shipment of money came from the east, and Alaina reasoned that any rebuilding effort at the smelter would not begin until spring thaw. A day of leisure and an early start the next morning would possibly save them time in the long run, for they and the horses would be well-rested for the next leg of the journey. Alaina was almost certain they could reach Baggs in two day's worth of hard riding. From there, it would be another two days to Encampment.

The first item of business for the day was a leisurely breakfast in the hotel café. Afterward, feeling as if they couldn't possibly eat again for a week, Alaina led the way to the mercantile she had noticed the previous evening. She purchased a complete change of clothes for each of them, including undergarments, shirts, split skirts and a hat for Rose. Then she bought another bedroll for Rose, as well. They had been sharing the blankets in Alaina's bedroll, which had left each of them shivering at times.

She replenished their supplies for the remainder of the journey, including coffee and tin cups for the trail. She had forgotten how much she missed a hot cup of strong coffee to drive the chill away in the dawning of the morning.

* * *

For the next two hours, they pampered themselves with a hot bath and a real shampoo back at the hotel, after which they each donned their new outfits and laundered the old ones in order to have a clean change later. The afternoon slipped away with the girls relaxing and enjoying the town. Not that there was much happening, but the idea that they were among other people in a civilized environment brought the girls a certain feeling of security and contentment. They checked on the horses before nightfall and then had another go at the hotel café before returning to their room for a good night's sleep and an early start in the morning.

* * *

The well-traveled trail along the Yampa River made progress seem almost too easy considering what they had been dealing with since leaving the cave almost a week before. The river valley was deep and wide with sheer cliffs rising high on either side. The valley floor along the river was rich with wildlife. Alaina knew that was because of the deep snow in the surrounding mountains. Food and water were much more plentiful along the river valley.

After another good breakfast before leaving the hotel, both girls were ready to make up some time. They had a new supply of jerky to satisfy any need for energy as they traveled. By mid-afternoon, they had reached a fork in the river that Alaina took to be the Snake. Turning northeast along their new route, they agreed to continue as long as there was light enough to see. The mountains were covered with snow, and a full moon soon appeared over the eastern horizon lighting the valley almost like daylight.

Alaina broke the silence. "If we keep going, we might make Baggs before midnight. What do you think?"

"*Si*," Rose replied, "*Bueno.*"

They pushed on, stopping periodically to rest and water the horses. Alaina expected Baggs, Wyoming, to appear as they rounded every bend in the river, but the moon trekked across the sky with no town in sight. She had been considering making camp when a line of dark clouds snuffed out the moon, and in a matter of minutes, large snowflakes began floating lazily down upon them.

Finding a sheltered spot among some pines and large boulders, they quickly set up camp, dragging up wood and starting a fire and gathering pine boughs for a pad for their bedrolls. Alaina hobbled the mare and allowed Badger to roam free, knowing they wouldn't go far, especially as tired as they must be. They gave them each a portion of grain from Frank's saddlebag before crawling into their bedrolls and pulling the blankets over their heads to shield themselves from any flakes that might filter down through the trees.

The girls spent a restless night, taking turns tending the fire. Daylight revealed a fresh blanket of snow with a fine powder still coming down. They brewed a pan of coffee and made do on jerky and leftover biscuits from the café back in Vernal, then hurriedly broke camp and continued on their way.

By what she calculated to be mid-morning, Alaina began to have an uneasy feeling. *Surely they should have reached Baggs by now,* she thought. She wished the clouds would break so she could get a bearing on their direction. They were traveling upstream, so common sense told her they had to either be going east or north, for they were west of the Continental Divide, and west of the Continental Divide rivers and streams run west or south.

The farther into the day, the more certain she felt that something was wrong. The clouds hung near to the ground, at times shrouding even the walls of the canyon along the river. It was impossible to tell the time of day or their direction, being unfamiliar with the landscape. Soon the sky began to grow dim and then dark. Alaina finally broke the long silence.

"Something is wrong. We should have been to Baggs long ago," Alaina explained.

"*Si*, I think so," Rose agreed.

Alaina continued, "I don't know where we are, but we have no choice but to keep going now. To turn back to that last fork in the river would take another day. Eventually the sun will have to show, and I can get us going in the right direction. We may as well make camp here."

* * *

The following morning proved to be everything the girls had hoped for. The storm had passed during the night and stars covered the sky as dawn began to break in the river valley. They made coffee and chewed on jerky while gathering everything together to continue on their way.

The eastern sky began to grow brighter as the sun prepared to peak over the horizon, and just as Alaina had suspected, the river valley they had been following was taking them north to northwest instead of northeast. The sheer cliffs on both sides of the river would make it almost impossible to head east from their current location, so Alaina and Rose agreed they should continue following the river upstream for a while longer.

About mid-morning, the river valley began to widen, and a short time later a cabin appeared in the distance. When they rode into the barnyard of the little homestead, a young couple came out to meet them. After a short exchange, the girls learned that the river they had taken wasn't the Snake but the Green, and in fact, had brought them north to Green River, Wyoming.

A discomforting feeling stole over Alaina as she realized they had accidently arrived back onto the route of the rail system across Wyoming. She had wanted to steer clear of every possible chance of bumping into the men responsible for Rose's horrible experience. There was one good side to the situation, however, she could telegraph her parents and inform them where she was and of her intentions.

It had been a cold, tiring journey from Vernal. *A good warm bed and hot meal will do wonders for our spirits*, Alaina thought. She was still irritated with herself about taking the wrong turn. *I should have followed my instincts and just continued traveling cross-country. Trying to use that blasted river to guide me was a mistake.*

If they had gone straight from Vernal to Green River, it would have only taken one hard day's ride. Instead, they had been following rivers all through the godforsaken country for almost four days.

Oh well, that's water under the bridge, she thought, as she resigned herself to make the best of the situation.

Green River, Wyoming, was named for the river on whose bank it was situated. It was a sizable town with several streets crisscrossing one another between the railroad and the river. Alaina and Rose agreed they should get to the telegraph office before anything else distracted them. By now, Alaina's mother and father would be beside themselves with worry.

As they approached the train depot and the Western Union office, a westbound train was sitting on the siding track waiting for an eastbound to clear the way so it could continue westward. Alaina wondered how long it had taken to get everything back on schedule and running smoothly after the rockslide and derailment she had witnessed several weeks ago.

It took only a few minutes to send the two telegrams and get directions to the livery stable and a hotel. Once the horses were cared for, they turned their attention to their own comforts.

Alaina and Rose found the hotel near the center of town and rented a room for the night, then went to the café for a well-deserved meal. As they ate, they talked about what they should do now that they were north of their intended route to Encampment. There were two options according to their discussion. One was to take a train to Rawlins and ride south and east to Battle and then to Encampment. The other was to ride from Green River in a south easterly direction across the mountains to Battle and then to Encampment.

The first option would get them there much quicker and with less hardship for the horses. The only benefit of the latter option would be to stay clear of the populated areas for Rose's safety. For this reason, Alaina told Rose that she could decide which route they would take. She had until nine o'clock the following morning to come to a final decision, for that was when the next eastbound train was scheduled to leave Green River.

Caught up in their own conversation and the delicious meal before them, neither of the girls paid attention to the other customers in the crowded café. However, across the room seated at a table in the farthest corner, two men were paying particular attention to them. Sudden recognition prompted them to slide their chairs around in order to place their backs toward the young ladies on the far side of the café.

The afternoon slipped lazily away as the two girls spent most of it lounging in their room. They waited until late in the evening to visit the café again, where they enjoyed a leisurely meal and the warm comforts of civilization, possibly for the last time…for a while, at least. A time or two during the evening, Alaina felt a slight chill down the back of her neck and an eerie sensation she sometimes got when she felt there was danger lurking. Each time she would stop and peruse their surroundings, noting nothing out of the ordinary, so she concluded that her imagination was running wild.

Rose finally revealed that, in her opinion, they should take the train to Rawlins the next morning. She felt it would not only be better for the horses, but it would get them to Encampment several days sooner. Alaina agreed with the decision, adding that they would have to be very careful in their investigation when they arrived in Encampment so as not to give away any information concerning the intended heist of the investment funds that were to be transferred there. However, she had no idea how they could gain the information they needed without divulging what Rose had heard in that meeting in Coalville months before.

The big clock over the ticket window of the train depot showed a few minutes before eight the following morning as Alaina finished with arrangements for a stock car for the horses and passage for two in a coach from Green River to Rawlins. Their stock car was assigned, and the ticket master directed them to its location and gave them permission to go ahead and load their horses. The Conductor would assure that their car was both hooked up at Green River and dropped off in the yard at Rawlins.

They found the car with no problem. The two sliding doors were open and the ramp was already lowered, so they led the horses inside and ran the reins through tie rings that were attached to the framework of the car. Alaina was about to portion out some grain from the saddle bag that their generous friend, Frank, had given them when she heard a gasping sound from behind her.

She turned to see Rose backing toward the corner of the stock car and two large figures silhouetted in the doorway. Although she had never seen the one man, she immediately recognized the other as the one who had proposed to be the sheriff at Coalville on that snowy night that now seemed so long ago.

The two men split up, one coming for each of the girls. Fear had altogether overcome Rose. She crumpled to the floor in the corner whimpering like a child, covering her face with her hands as if to ward off the blows she thought were coming. Alaina, however, was not about to come under submission so easily.

The big man came for her in a rush. She was blocked from the door, but she tried to dodge around him with no success. He wrapped his huge muscular arms around her and lifted her feet off the floor in a bearhug fashion. Her arms were pinned helplessly to her sides, but she began kicking frantically with her feet, connecting with the burley man's shins in a relentless volley from the pointed toes of her western-type riding boots.

After a few minutes of failure to subdue the attack on his legs, the man threw Alaina violently to the floor of the car. As she lunged upward to attempt escape again, she saw a huge fist coming toward her face with all the power and might the man had in him.

* * *

Alaina's first conscious thought was, *why can I not move my arms and legs?* Her next was, *what is this excruciating pain in my cheek and jaw?* Her eyes gradually opened to bring her to a full awareness of their grave situation.

She was lying on her side on the floor of the stock car with her hands and feet pulled behind her and bound tightly together. The car was only dimly lit by the dusky, shadowy coming of nightfall, but she could see that Rose lay in a similar heap in the corner where she had immediately cowered from the sight of her worst enemy. Both girls were hopelessly bound and gagged, but Alaina began to try to speak, if only to learn if Rose was conscious. She gave a sigh of relief when Rose mumbled some unrecognizable response.

The stock car rocked from side to side as the train moved along at a smart pace. Alaina began to attempt to loosen the ropes around her wrists. She had become near expert at freeing herself from her father's knots and loops.

She had heard the story many times of how he had freed himself and saved both his and his mother's lives when he was a child. He accredited the feat to the games between him and his father and carried on the tradition with Alaina. They had spent hours on cold winter nights tying one another with their best techniques and then timing each other with her father's pocket watch to see who could get free in the quickest time.

As she writhed and twisted, trying desperately to force some slack in her present bindings, she soon realized that her father had been too lenient in tying his knots. These ropes would not budge. She began to mumble to Rose and motion for her to try to position themselves with their backs together. After repeated attempts and some effort, they managed to achieve their purpose, and Alaina set to work on the knots that bound Rose's hands and feet.

She was soon interrupted by the startling scream of the train whistle and a noticeable slowing as they began to approach a station. Alaina had no way of knowing where they were exactly, for she did not know how long she had been unconscious. The train always stopped at the Rock Springs depot, no matter if there were no passengers to board or depart, but there were several small settlements between Rock Springs and Rawlins where they might stop if there was a signal out. If there was no signal, then they would simply slow their speed and pass on by.

However, since it was now dark outside, she estimated that they should be nearing their destination of Rawlins. She continued to work frantically on the knots and soon began to feel them loosening. With a little more effort, the first knot came free, and soon she had Rose's hands completely untied. Rose quickly freed Alaina's hands, and the two of them then worked on the bindings on their feet.

The train had come to a complete stop by now and began a constant lurching back and forth, which told the girls they were either hooking or unhooking cars. Alaina quickly moved to the sliding doors and grabbing the handle of the one nearest her, she threw her weight against it in an attempt to crack it open enough to see outside. To her dismay, the door would not budge.

She called for Rose's help and the two of them pushed and pulled with all of their strength with no success. Alaina assumed they were fastened somehow from the outside. There were several half inch cracks here and there that allowed them to peek through, but hardly adequate to tell what was going on outside.

After several cycles of moving forward and then backward, they realized the train had moved away, leaving their car sitting. Both girls began to yell out for help from anyone who might be within the sound of their voice but with no luck. After a few minutes, the train whistle blew again, and they listened as it rumbled off into the night.

The girls continued to struggle with the door for several minutes with no success. Rose began to tell Alaina about the conversation she had overheard as the men discussed plans to get rid of them. The one who pretended to be a sheriff told the other one to go with the train and stand watch over the box car and to make sure no one came near it. Meanwhile, he would return to a place called Brown's Hole to get more help for their job. He said that he would be back to Rawlins tomorrow night and they would finish the girls then.

Alaina suddenly stopped pulling on the door. "So that means the one who was the mayor at Coalville is watching this car right now?" Alaina asked.

"*Sí*, I think so," Rose replied.

Alaina looked toward her saddle. Strangely enough, they had not thought about her having a saddle gun…or perhaps they thought there was no chance that either of them could work free of the ropes. The rifle remained in its scabbard.

Alaina immediately retrieved it and checked the magazine for cartridges. Seeing it was full, she motioned for Rose to join her as she backed into one corner of the stock car. They huddled there through the night, taking turns keeping watch and napping when they could.

Alaina hadn't stopped thinking about their situation all night long. An idea had begun to form, and as dawn broke, she was able to look through the small cracks in the sliding doors. She could see what looked to be links in a chain. She explained to Rose what her intentions were. It would take teamwork and coordination between the two of them, but it was their only chance to escape.

They untied the horses and prepared them for a quick getaway. Then Alaina jacked a shell into the chamber of her saddle gun. She made another quick inspection of the position of the chain that ran through the outside door handles and told Rose to stand well out of the way of the horses in case they were startled by the rifle shots.

Placing the muzzle of the gun against one of the small cracks, she pointed it in the direction of the chain and pulled the trigger. Without hesitation, she continued pumping shells and pulling the trigger. The bullets tore through the wood of the door, enlarging the crack and striking the links of the chain over and over. When Alaina hesitated long enough to look through the hole made by the bullets, she realized that only a small piece of steel remained holding one of the links of the chain together.

She took aim and pulled the trigger once again and watched the chain fall apart and slide to the ground outside. Quickly, she and Rose pushed the doors apart and slid the deadbolts that fastened the ramp in place, allowing it to fall to the ground. Each of them scrambled for the saddle, looked at one another to be sure they were ready, and in unison the two horses bolted from the stock car and raced across the train yard to the street beyond.

Alaina looked back over her shoulder as they rounded the corner of the depot and saw the mayor of Coalville, Utah running after them. He had no gun in his hand—just a look of exasperated disbelief as he watched the girls ride away.

* * *

The two young riders wasted no time clearing out of town. Alaina knew the route to Encampment by way of the little settlements of Dillon and Battle and soon led them south out of Rawlins on the old Sage Creek Road. Both Dillon and Battle had sprung up as a result of the mining operations in the area. The most successful was the Ferris-Haggerty Copper Mine, which prompted the building of the copper smelter plant in Encampment.

The copper ore, at 33% copper, was rich enough to pay workers and still generate a profit but not a large enough profit to keep the investors satisfied. The ore had to be meticulously hauled down across the Continental Divide to the plant below by wagon and team. Sometimes as many as 20 horses or mules would be required to maneuver the treacherous decent.

Alaina had learned all about the entire operation through her mother who had been retained by the mine co-op to represent them in a court action brought upon them by a group of the investors who claimed fraudulent actions on the part of the Board of Directors. The Board of Directors contended that the slow process by which the ore had to be transported to the smelter was the reason for the meager return on investment money; therefore, they had devised a new campaign strategy to raise more money. They were trying to lead investors to believe that they would all be rich in a matter of a few years if they would stay the course and build a fourteen-mile tramway from the mine to the smelter.

A light suddenly came on in Alaina's head. She thought that perhaps they had succeeded in selling the investors on the plan. Perhaps that was the reason for the supposed influx of a large amount of money into the little town of Encampment, Wyoming, and not just renovation. That would require a large sum, indeed. As always, when large amounts of money were changing hands, there were those waiting in the shadows to try to arrange for it to change into their hands.

It really meant nothing to Alaina, other than the fact that her mother was somewhat invested in the cause to see to the success of the smelter. Another fact was that the law was about to be broken and her family was all about the enforcement of the law on everyone's behalf. Her mother and father both insisted that if no one cared about the law, the entire country would quickly go to the dogs. Besides, both she and Rose had a score to settle now.

Her cheek and jaw smarted with every hoof beat and served as a constant reminder of that. She remembered reading in the Good Book that vengeance belonged to the Lord, but she couldn't help but feel that Rose had a right to at least a little bit of vengeance for what that scoundrel of a man had done to her and her brother.

Dillon, Wyoming, was located a few miles from the mine and consisted of nothing more than a store, a newspaper and a bar room with a few tables for gambling cards. About two dozen or so shacks had been thrown together with logs and planks and topped off with either tin or cedar shingles to be used as makeshift lodging for some of the miners.

Both girls had ridden in silence the entire morning, each lost in their own thoughts. Alaina was concerned about Rose. The reappearance of her archenemy had shaken her immensely. She hadn't been herself since the encounter in the stockcar.

Alaina finally broke the silence as they entered the little village. "Let's stop in at the little store and see if we can learn anything. The storekeeper will have heard any gossip about the mine or smelter."

"*Si,*" Rose responded.

They dismounted at the hitch rail, each one glad for a break from the saddle. Alaina looked up and down the street before entering the store, more out of habit than anything but determined not to be blindsided again. She saw nothing out of the ordinary and no one looked suspicious, so she followed Rose inside. Half a dozen people went about their business collecting articles and the supplies they had come for. Alaina and Rose moved among them inspecting merchandise as if considering whether to buy. They overheard nothing but small talk from the customers, so Alaina went to the counter and struck up a conversation with the clerk.

"My friend and I are involved in a special project at the girl's school over in Laramie," she began. "We're doing research on the Haggerty Mine and on the smelter plant in Encampment. What we need is to get firsthand information about how the entire enterprise actually works. We tried to gain a hearing with the plant manager at the smelter, but he was too busy to waste his time with a couple of young girls. Truth is, if we don't get our research paper turned in by this weekend, we will be given a failing grade in the class, which will likely cause us to fail the entire school year. We were wondering if these miners talk much about how things really work…I mean, with the management and everything."

The store clerk looked to be near thirty. He seemed to be a man of some education, although not a college man by any means. Alaina noticed him hitch up his trousers with an authoritative air.

"Well," he began, "I can possibly be of service in that area. I talk to just about everybody who is involved with the mine and the smelter plant. Know all the management on first-name basis. As a matter of fact, most all of 'em are what I consider close friends. What is it exactly that you want to know?"

"Mostly, we need to know how the financing is worked out. We've been told by some that the money that is generated by the copper that can be produced isn't really enough to keep things running. There are rumors that the entire operation is in danger of shutting down. We were wondering if the workers have been voicing any concern about losing their jobs."

Upon hearing that, the store clerk leaned across the counter and lowered his voice. "Not anymore," he offered. "Word around camp is that the worries are over, at least for a while. Money comin' in this week for a big project to carry the ore down the mountain. Nothin' like it has ever been done in this country. The place is buzzin' with excitement about it. Some kind of cable car system is what I hear. There's supposed to be some big wigs from back east and some from over in London, England, comin' in on the train to personally deliver the cash to finance the job. Maybe you could use that information in yer paper, huh?"

"We surely can!" Alaina agreed, purposely showing excitement. "But exactly how soon will the money be available to begin the work? Does anyone know?"

"Well, not exactly, but for sure within the next two weeks is what everybody says. The idea is to start to work right on the heels of spring thaw."

"Thank you so much. You have saved our lives. If we get a top grade on our paper we will be sure to tell our schoolmaster who is responsible," Alaina told him as she reached across the counter and patted the man's hand softly.

The clerk rewarded her praise with a smile from ear to ear as he responded, "You and your friend are mighty welcome, and if you need any more help on that paper, you just let ole Jase know. Name's James, but folks just started calling me Jase, and I guess it stuck."

Alaina looked at Rose and nodded toward the door. The minute they were mounted and moving toward Battle, Alaina began to explain what their next move must be.

"If there is an envoy coming to Encampment, they will most likely quit the train at Walcott Junction. That is due north of Encampment, and there's a stage that runs between the two. We have to get there ahead of that train, and its seventy miles from here, and the first twenty miles are a doozie of a ride."

9. Chasing a Ghost

Tall and Sheriff Frost led their weary horses down the main street of Rock Springs, Wyoming, to the livery stable they had spotted as they entered town a few hours before. Their first item of business had been to find a café for their first warm meal in almost a week. They had scoured the country from Coalville, Utah, to Encampment, Wyoming, where Butch had said there was something about to go down. When there was no sign of Alaina, they backtracked to Rock Springs, crisscrossing the entire area. They still had found no trace of her.

Tall checked back with Harvey Jenson at Wells Flats near the ranch from every telegraph office they came near, but Harvey had received no word from Alaina. However, he had learned that Cat had returned from San Francisco as soon as she received word about Alaina being overdue in coming home.

Tall felt a little guilty that he had been remiss in not telling his wife the whole story about Alaina's encounter with the outlaw sheriff in Coalville. In fact, he had been negligent from the start in not telling her how concerned he was about Alaina's failure to get home in a reasonable time. When he left to look for Alaina, he had hoped to locate her and save his wife from the anxiety of even knowing she was missing.

Cat had known from the very start, though, that something was terribly wrong, just as he had. She hadn't waited for word from him but took the first available train east and back home. In their first communication by telegraph, Cat had insisted on coming to help in the search, but Tall had been able to convince her that she should stay at the ranch and check regularly with Jens at Wells Flats in case there was news from Alaina.

After getting the horses settled into a nice stall with plenty of hay and double portions of grain, the two men went back to the hotel and arranged for a room. It was not even sundown yet, but they both agreed that it was dark enough to start with, and within a matter of minutes they were sleeping like dead men.

The room was bright with sunlight when Tall opened his eyes. When he checked the pocket watch on the table beside the bed, it showed a little after ten o'clock. He chuckled to himself as he swung his feet to the floor and began to get dressed. His movement immediately aroused Marc, and after washing up, they agreed that a good breakfast was in the cards for the two of them.

There was nothing like a strong pot of hot coffee to get a man back on his feet. Of course, the plate covered with ham and eggs, biscuits and gravy did not hurt anything either. Tall and Marc left the café and walked the quarter of a mile to the train depot and telegraph office to check in with Harvey before deciding which direction to take from here. The agent had hardly finished tapping out Tall's telegram to Jens when the key began the dot-dot-dash rhythm of a message coming in. The agent scribbled on a message form until the key fell silent.

"Maybe this is what you've been waiting for," he said, as he handed the form to Tall.

First his face broke into a smile, and then he began to laugh as he handed the message to Marc, and after reading, he, too, joined in the jubilance. Jens had received a wire from Alaina at eight o'clock yesterday morning sent from Green River, fifteen miles away. The message stated that she was well, for her parents not to worry, and she would be home in a few days, if all went as planned.

No words needed to be spoken. Both Marc and Tall rushed out the door, headed for the livery stable. The horses had enjoyed a good rest, as well as a couple of good feedings. They were quick to respond as their riders nudged them into an easy canter headed west toward Green River.

Two hours later, Tall and Marc rode up to the train depot in Green River, Wyoming. Tall stepped from the saddle before Sassy had come to a complete stop, threw the reins over the hitch rail and hurried up the steps through the door. Seeing the station master behind the desk, he rushed to the ticket window and blurted out.

"Mister, I'm trying to locate my little girl. I have been on her trail for over two months, and I got a telegram from this office yesterday. She is about so high," he held his hand about the level of his eyes. "Long blond hair and blue eyes. Do you have any notion where she might be?"

"Well, no, I don't know where she might be at this moment, but if it was your girl I'm thinking of, she was back in here this morning and rented a stock car and booked passage for two in the Pullman from here to Rawlins."

"She *what?*" Tall questioned incredulously.

"Yes sir," the agent affirmed. "In fact, I can show you the number on the stock car that was assigned to her. Uh, yes, here it is, Number 4559, Union Pacific stockcar. The conductor hooked it up all right, but I cannot guarantee that the girls were on the train. I did see them load their horses though."

Tall stepped backward, trying to process the bombardment of information as Marc joined him at the desk.

"I swear to God," Tall directed to Marc, "If I ever catch up with that girl, I will lock her up in her room and throw away the key. Do you realize that she was on that eastbound train we passed an hour ago on our way here? Apparently, she has another girl traveling with her."

"Well, at least we're certain she has made it this far safely. Let's get to Rawlins and see if we can catch up to her there," Marc responded.

Tall turned back to the ticket window and inquired, "When is the next train going east?"

"Not 'till nine o'clock tomorrow morning," came the reply.

Tall looked at Marc and shook his head. "Dang the luck," he began. "If we leave now and ride hard all night and all day, we can get to Rawlins by mid-afternoon tomorrow. If we get a room and take the train tomorrow morning, we can get to Rawlins about dark tomorrow. The thing is, if we ride from here, the horses will be used up when we arrive in Rawlins. If we take the train, they will be fresh as we will. What do you think, old friend?"

"Well, I don't think there is a question," Marc replied. "My backside has calluses from chasin' that little scalawag of yours all over creation for the past two months. My deputy will probably challenge me in the coming election for sheriff and beat me since I have been away from my post all this time. That might be a blessing in disguise. Anyway, I don't think two hours is going to make that much difference in our arrival in Rawlins. Let's eat, sleep, and ride the train tomorrow."

Tall arranged for a stockcar and passage for two for the nine o'clock train the following day, and after caring for the horses, he and Marc went to the hotel for a meal and room for the night.

10. A PLAN COMES TOGETHER

Alaina and Rose had pushed Badger and the big bay mare hard all day. It was nearing sundown when they reached the Wolf Hotel in Saratoga. It was still at least three hours of hard riding to Walcott Junction, and with an overcast sky, Alaina knew it would be practically pitch black when darkness came.

The stage from Rawlins and Walcott Junction had just pulled up in front of the Wolf Hotel, which doubled as the local stage stop. The stage line from Rawlins to Encampment had once been a part of her father's enterprise, but ranching and horse breeding had claimed his main interest over the years, and he had sold the Jamis Johnson Overland Dispatch Company to a man named Scribner about five years ago. However, Alaina recognized the driver as the same man who had worked for her father for all the years he had owned the company.

John Jefferson Fulkerson was his name, but he had earned the nicknamed "G-String Jack" because of his unusual skill as a freight wagon driver. The heavy loads sometimes required as many as twenty-four horses to pull them over the rugged terrain, and the driver used what was called a jerk line or "G-string" to guide the front left lead horse.

"G-String Jack" had proven himself as the best there was for hauling heavy machinery. He also made it a point to keep informed about any and everything that had to do with the mine and smelter plant, for they were his bread and butter, so to speak. The old driver was just climbing down from the spring seat of the Concord stagecoach as Alaina and Rose approached the hitch rail in front of the hotel and stepped from their saddles.

"Good evening, Mr. Fulkerson," Alaina greeted. "Do you remember me?"

The driver looked her over for a long minute before speaking. "Naw, I don't 'spect I do, although you do have a familiarity about you."

"I'm Alaina…Tall Johnson's daughter."

"Well, by cracky, you've growed up since I've seed you last. Why, you weren't nothin' but a sprout last time I recollect you ridin' all over Wyomin' with yer ole daddy. What brings you to these parts and this late in the day?"

"My friend and I are just traveling through on our way home from Encampment." Alaina felt a twinge of guilt the minute she told him that untruth. She could not help it. To tell him what she was really doing in Saratoga, Wyoming, would not be good for anyone involved, him as well as herself and Rose.

She decided to go ahead with the big fabrication of fantasy that she had begun earlier in the day with the store clerk at Dillon. "Rose and I are doing some research for a school project concerning the copper mine and smelter plant. We have learned that they are going to expand their operation by building a cable system of some sort to bring the ore down from the mine to the smelter. I figured with you being involved with hauling their freight you would know about any plans for new equipment being shipped in."

The old driver stepped closer and toned his voice down a notch. "Well, sounds like you two have been doin' yer homework all right. Matter of fact, they's gonna be a lot of heavy haulin' startin' real soon."

Alaina stepped even closer and brought the conversation almost to a whisper.

"Well, have you heard about the envoy coming with the big shipment of money all the way from London?"

The old man's eyes widened in surprise. "Lordy mercy, girl, who in the world told you about that?" G-String Jack realized his mistake the minute the words came out and tried to cover it over. "Not that there's anything to all that gossip, mind you."

Alaina couldn't help but smile. She had him, and he knew it.

"You don't have to worry yourself, Mr. Fulkerson. We know all about it, but we are not about to divulge our information. We are sworn to secrecy, in fact, but I knew you would be aware of the itinerary of such important passengers with your stage being the most secure means of travel from Walcott Junction to Encampment and all."

Alaina noticed the old driver's chest swell a little with the compliment as she continued, "We have already made plans to be in Laramie when their train arrives next week. We are hoping to get to speak with the Englishman in person. Wouldn't that be a clincher for a perfect grade on our school project?" The driver smiled at that. Alaina had been fishing, and he took the bait again, hook, line, and sinker.

"Well, yer gonna hav'ta do some travelin' iffen you plan to go all the way to yer ranch and then back to Laramie afore Tuesday." G-String Jack said just above a whisper. "I'm due to pick 'um up at Walcott Wednesday mornin' early, so I figger they'll stay the night in Laramie, seein' as how they'll need to be concerned about protection, an' all.

"I had to look all over God's creation to find extra guards for that trip. Luck would have it they's a sheriff and his deputies jist arrived in Rawlins from over in Provo, Utah. They have to be in town for a few more days, anyways, so I managed to convince them to lend a hand ridin' guard for me and pick up a few extry bucks to help cover their expenses."

Alaina almost exploded in protest but managed to hold herself in check. She looked at Rose and realized from her expression that she, too, understood that the sheriff he spoke of was not from Provo and was not a real sheriff but was none other than the very man who had beaten her and left her for dead. Alaina gently shook her head from side to side, signaling her to keep silent.

"Well, you be careful Mr. Fulkerson," she cautioned. "We can't have you getting hurt."

"Awe now, don't you fret yerself 'bout me. I'm not 'spectin' trouble. Not very many people even know what's brewin' anyways," the old teamster replied.

"It's nice to see you again after all these years. I guess we'll have ourselves a good meal before we continue on."

With that exchange, the girls made their way into the hotel café. Alaina chose a table in the corner away from the other customers. She could hardly contain herself with the new information about the men who were hired to guard the envoy and the shipment of money.

As soon as they settled into their chairs, Alaina leaned across the table and spoke in almost a whisper. "We have to do something. If that money gets to Walcott, there is no way we can stop that mob from taking it. We can't go to the sheriff in Rawlins with our story. Chances are he wouldn't believe us against a sheriff from Utah and all of his deputies. We would also have to be concerned with those terrible men surprising us again. Next time they would be sure we did not get away. Our only chance is to get to Laramie before the envoy arrives and somehow intercept the money there. I think I have an idea. Let me consider it tonight while we rest the horses, and we'll get an early start for Laramie in the morning."

* * *

Alaina and Rose saddled up at the crack of dawn. The pass over the Sugarloaf Range to the east would be neck deep to a tall giraffe with snow, so Alaina had pointed them northeast, and by the time the sun began to show itself, Elk Mountain loomed before them. They would skirt around the north side of Elk Mountain and then turn east to Laramie. If they kept the pace that each of their mounts had become accustomed to, they should arrive in Laramie by nightfall.

There were no settlements across the broad expanse of plains and foothills, so each of the girls settled in for a long, hard day in the saddle, stopping only to rest the horses and give them a refreshing drink from a cold mountain stream and an occasional handful of grain from the saddlebag. The south facing mountain slopes, being exposed to the sun most of the day, had begun to produce a few sprigs of green grass, a well-deserved treat for the faithful mounts.

Rose had named the big mare Amiga, or "girlfriend," in Spanish. She had certainly proven herself to be a friend. Both girls realized how fortunate they had been to have two strong horses for all the travels they had been doing over snow-covered mountains in the wintertime.

By mid-afternoon, Alaina realized they had made much better time than she had anticipated, for the mountains east of Laramie began to show themselves in the distance. When she estimated they had only a few miles to go, they slowed the horses to a walk to allow them to cool down before reaching her grandparents' ranch just across the river west of town. George and Edna Gray were her great-grandparents really, but they had raised her mother, who was their granddaughter, as their own child, and Alaina like a grandchild, thus Alaina considered them to be her grandparents.

Alaina had given a great deal of thought to the situation with the money and the outlaw gang that would be waiting at Walcott Junction. If she and Rose allowed the money to get that far, Alaina felt sure there would be killing involved. The so-called sheriff from Coalville, Utah, had murdered before, and she was certain he would not hesitate to do it again. They could not just take the money themselves. The last thing she needed was to be found guilty of robbery and placed in the federal penitentiary. There was a federal pen right here in Laramie and there were gruesome tales about what happened to the prisoners in that godforsaken place.

As they covered the last mile to the G Bar G ranch, Alaina explained to Rose what she had in mind. Rose agreed it would be risky but that it was probably the only way to prevent the money from being stolen and lives to be lost. She also agreed that the fewer people who were wise to their plan the better the chance of it being successful, so the two of them agreed to tell no one the truth. Instead, they cooked up what they thought would be a believable story for Alaina's grandparents.

George and Edna Gray were thrilled to learn that Alaina was safe and sound and was finally home again. Alaina's mother had kept them informed during the long absence. After introducing Rose, Alaina explained that she hadn't yet had a chance to telegraph her mother about her safe arrival in Laramie and that she just needed to get a few articles of clothing and be on her way home. She assured them that she would come back for a long visit after things returned to normal at the ranch.

She often spent time with them when she was in Laramie and had her own room and an entire wardrobe in her closet upstairs, as well as a buggy and team for travel in fine fashion when she needed them. Her grandmother, Deborah, her father's mother, also lived in Laramie. She and her Papa Jules ran a mercantile store.

Alaina wanted to try to not bump into either of them until their plan was carried out. She had already been more deceitful in the past two days than all the rest of her life put together, and she didn't want to have to lie to them, as well. She felt that she would already have a lot to answer for when she saw her parents—especially after what she and Rose were about to attempt to do. If it all worked out, she would be exonerated, but if not, well, she did not want to think about that right now.

After gathering up her favorite evening dress and shoes and other paraphernalia to dress to the hilt, she and Rose tied Badger and Amiga to the back of the buggy, threw in an extra saddle and bridle from the tack shed, hitched up one of the geldings that was broke to both saddle and harness and drove into Laramie. They stabled all three horses and acquired a room in the hotel that was nearest the train depot, and Alaina asked specifically for a room on the north side of the hotel. She wanted to have a clear view of the rail station from the hotel window.

Upon entering the room, she hung the evening dress in the closet and then walked the short distance to the depot and sent a telegram to her parents, one to her mother, whom she guessed was still in San Francisco, and one to her father at the ranch. She only told them that she was in Laramie and on her way to the ranch.

Another little white lie added to the long list, she thought, *but justified, because it had some truth to it, and the full truth would only cause them to worry more.*

She also told her father that she needed his help with something when she arrived. Before leaving the depot, she learned from the station master that the next scheduled train coming from the east would arrive at six o'clock the following evening.

Ole G-String Jack had it figured right, she thought to herself. *If the envoy were on that train, they would be staying tomorrow night here in Laramie.*

* * *

Alaina and Rose were up before dawn preparing for the day while no one was moving around on the street. After hooking the gelding to the carriage, they saddled the other two horses and tied them to the back, then threw an extra saddle, bridle and blankets into the seat. Rose would drive the carriage to Medicine Bow and spend the night there. The following morning, she would position the buggy for Alaina. Then she would hide the horses and the extra saddle in a location Alaina described to her and wait for Alaina's arrival on the same train that would carry the envoy of financiers.

As soon as Rose was on her way to Medicine Bow, Alaina purchased a train ticket for herself for the following morning and then went back to the hotel room to keep out of site for the rest of the day. She arranged for her meals to be served in her room so as not to bump into any of her many acquaintances in Laramie, especially her Grandma Deb or Papa Jules.

The day dragged by like molasses in January, but when the sun finally began to sink toward the west, Alaina pulled a chair up to the windowsill where she had positioned her binoculars on the ledge. She heard the whistle before the engine came into view around the last curve in the track, already slowing almost to a stop as it positioned the one Pullman car next to the landing. Normal passenger traffic usually only required one passenger coach and Alaina was glad that was the case now. It would greatly simplify the plan she had in mind.

Alaina trained her binoculars on the door of the car and watched as the passengers began to exit onto the landing. She watched them step down one by one without any obvious agent or envoy among them. She had begun to think their plan was shot, that the money wasn't on this train and they would have to regroup and plan for the next one, when a man in a dark blue suit stepped out of the car followed by two more in similar attire and one more in a light brown business suit that reminded Alaina of the gentlemen she remembered seeing in the magazines from France and England.

The three men in the blue suits wore shield-shaped badges on the lapels of their coats. The first man also had another badge, a star, pinned to his suit coat below the shield. He paused as he reached the platform and looked all around for any sign of trouble before waving for the others to follow.

The second man, the only one in the light brown suit, was noticeably young. Alaina guessed him to be no more than twenty. He was taller than the others and broad through the shoulders. He had sandy hair that looked to be well-groomed but different from any style Alaina had ever seen; it was parted right down the middle and brushed back on the sides. The style of his suit was different also, as were his shoes. He held a cane in his left hand that boasted a gold, knob-like crest on the top and gold tip on the other end. In his right hand was a large leather bag.

He is the one from London, Alaina said to herself. *Wow, I wonder if all young Englishmen are as dashing as this one!*

She felt herself blush and consciously moved the binoculars from his pleasing facial features to the large leather bag. It bulged at the sides, and seemed to be particularly heavy, judging by the way he leaned to one side as he walked.

That's it, she thought. *That's the money!*

She watched the four men walk across the street in a tight huddle until they reached the bank. The door swung open as they approached, and they filed inside. Alaina realized that every small detail had been carefully planned. Even the bank that would normally have been closed for the day had been notified as to the exact time the money would arrive and had someone waiting to receive it. The train that normally would have continued on westward was moved onto a side track to resume its journey the following day.

Well, her work was done for now. She could relax until morning. Then, she reflected, her life could take an abrupt change in direction. She said a little prayer as she readied her articles of dress for tomorrow. She checked the gown, hat, shoes, and handbag to make sure they were perfect. She took the small derringer from the handbag, broke it down, and once again made sure that both barrels were loaded. As she placed each one back in its place, a knock at the door told her that her supper had arrived.

11. STILL CHASING A GHOST

Tall and Marc stood at the door of the Pullman waiting for the train to roll to a stop in Rawlins, Wyoming. The instant the porter pulled it open, they hurried to the stock car to unload their horses. They led them to the hitch rail in front of the depot, and Tall took his place in the line waiting to get to the ticket window. He reached the window in only a few minutes.

The ticket master finished placing money in the cash drawer from the previous customer and looked up as he spoke. "How can I help you?" he asked mechanically.

"My daughter rode the evening train from Green River to this station yesterday. She booked passage for two and rented a stock car for two horses. Here's the number on the stock car she rented." He flashed the paper with the number that the ticket master in Green River had provided in front of him. "There's evidently another young girl traveling with her. I need to know if you saw them, and if so, can you tell me where they might be?"

"So, that was your daughter?" the man began. "Yes, I saw her. I saw her racing off across the tracks like the devil hisself was after her. And that was directly after I heard a bunch a gunfire coming from the direction of that there stock car." He pointed out the window as he spoke. "She shot up the door on that car, by the way. Some feller went runnin' after um on foot, but they was gone in a flash." He was chuckling now. "As far as knowin' where they were headed or where they are now, I don't."

After hearing the man's explanation of the previous evening's excitement, Marc turned instantly and went to the stock car to poke around to see what he could discover.

Tall was still trying to sort through the information he'd just been given. "I need to send a telegram to Harvey Jenson at the Union Pacific office at the village up north of Medicine Bow called Wells Flats. Just ask if he has heard from Alaina Johnson. I'll wait for a reply."

Tall left the office and went to the stock car where Marc was still looking around. He had lifted the loading ramp, and when Tall walked up, he pointed to a broken chain lying on the ground.

"That chain was shot apart. There's spent cartridges and a bunch of rope bindings in the floor. Looks like someone had been tied up and the door chained shut. Guess we know who it was."

Tall went back to the ticket window. "Did those two girls honor their tickets to ride the Pullman from Green River?" he asked pointedly.

"There's no indication that they did," the ticket master replied. "The porter on board rode the train on down the line to Laramie, but their tickets are not among those he turned in here."

As he spoke, the telegraph key began to tap out a message. "This is for you," he said as he began jotting on a writing pad. He brought the paper to him when he had finished. Tall read it and hurried toward the door.

"Thanks," he said. "This tells me what I need to know."

He whistled to Marc as he stepped out onto the landing. "Alaina just arrived in Laramie," he said, as Marc approached. "She's on her way home. We may as well book passage to Medicine Bow."

12. Dancing with the Devil

Alaina woke with a start and sat upright in bed. The little clock on the desk showed five o'clock. She had slept fitfully, lying awake for long intervals, going over and over in her mind how she would carry out her plan the next day. The train would not leave for three more hours, but she couldn't lie there any longer.

She had chosen this hotel because it was near the train depot, but it was also the newest in town and had all the modern conveniences, including bath facilities in every room. A giant wood-burning boiler located out back even supplied hot running water. Alaina drew a bath and made use of the fragrant, bubbly body soap that the hotel maid had placed for her on the lavatory counter. Her stomach seemed to be tied in knots. Breakfast was out of the question, so she decided to use the extra time to relax and try to rid herself of the butterflies that kept her wondering if she might have to be sick.

She could not remember anything causing her to feel so uneasy. Of course, she had never attempted anything so dangerous and daring as her plan would require of her today. Over and over in her mind she reviewed every move she would make, every word she would say, and exactly what expression she would reveal as she readied herself for the train ride.

She took particular care in fixing her hair, placing the stylish hat at just the right tilt on her head, blushing her cheeks and darkening the red of her lips ever so slightly. She had "borrowed" some of her mother's cosmetics while gathering up the other things she needed. When she felt satisfied that she had done everything possible to acquire the look she was after, she rose from the vanity and gathered up her one piece of luggage and her handbag, checking it again to be sure the derringer was still there. If everything went as planned, she wouldn't need to use it, but she felt better knowing it was there and ready…just in case.

She took one last look in the mirror before leaving the room. She smiled ever so slightly, happy with the result of her transformation. The fashionable young lady peering back at her looked to be at least twenty years of age.

Alaina hurried to the train depot, hoping she would not be recognized by anyone. The train had been moved back to the main track and had just rolled up to the platform as she climbed the steps to the landing. She quickly moved to the end of the line of passengers at the door of the Pullman and presented her ticket to the porter. Moving inside, she surveyed the passengers and the available seating. She chose a position next to two other seats that remained empty as she looked anxiously across the street toward the bank.

"Why don't they hurry up?" she mumbled to herself.

A middle-aged lady moved down the aisle, inspecting the two empty seats that Alaina had purposefully positioned herself next to. Alaina instantly went into action.

"I'm sorry, Miss, but these seats are reserved for the four gentlemen coming there." She had spied them moving across the street from the bank in the nick of time. "As you can see, they are a special envoy and require seating all together," Alaina added.

The lady looked toward the four men for assurance that Alaina was telling her the truth and then moved to another empty seat farther back. The four men made their way to where Alaina was seated, and to her extreme satisfaction, the young English gentleman took a seat directly across and facing her.

Perfect! she thought to herself. *Now to somehow gain his interest.*

For the first time, Alaina noticed the handcuffs. They did not look like the cuffs that Sheriff Frost carried. She guessed they were English made. One of the restraints was fastened to the young gentleman's wrist while the other encircled both handles of the large leather bag he carried. A length of chain secured the two together.

Good, she thought. *It goes where he goes.*

The young man placed the bag on the seat between himself and the wall of the Pullman and settled back in his seat. He looked across the few feet of space separating the two of them and looked directly into Alaina's eyes. Instantly his countenance changed.

Alaina recognized a spark of interest as his expression softened and a slight smile curled the corners his mouth. She felt her face blush as her heart began to pound so loudly she was sure he must be able to hear it also. She tried to contain her composure without a hint of any evidence of the excitement she felt, but she had not taken into consideration what happened next.

"I say, Miss," the young gentleman spoke, addressing Alaina. "Might I say you look extremely ravishing considering the early hour of the morning?" He paused, taking in her reaction toward his boldness and then continued in his thick English brogue. "Might I introduce myself? I am John Christopher Braunche, and may I be so bold as to say that I have traveled from London to New York City and across the entire broad expanse of these United States to what I had come to believe was the most awful wasteland I would ever encounter only to find my day has been brightened by a most beautiful flower of the desert."

Alaina sat speechless. She suddenly became aware that her mouth had dropped open. Her cheeks burned with a new rush from her pounding heart. She recovered quickly and smiled at him ever so slightly, trying hard to imitate the women of society she had observed at the balls and gatherings she had attended with her mother from time to time.

The Englishman continued the one-sided conversation. "If you would allow my being so forward as to inquire, for what distance will we be honored with your company?"

"Only to Medicine Bow," Alaina forced herself to reply in a manner that practically dripped with honey, as she smiled again and lowered her gaze purposely toward the floor of the coach.

Everything is going perfectly, Alaina mused. *If only Rose will be ready and do her part, we just might pull this thing off.*

Alaina was aware that the gaze of the young English gentleman, John Christopher, was turned in her direction from time to time. She made it a point to occasionally glance his way and smile ever so faintly, just enough for him to notice. She was careful though, to stay focused on the progress of the train.

They only slowed for the little village of Bowler, but when they came to Rock River, the porter announced that the train would be stopping but only for a moment and that all passengers should remain seated. He then explained that the next stop at Medicine Bow would be for half an hour and would provide enough time for passengers to disembark for refreshments. He added that the hotel in Medicine Bow offered a fine café and that it would be the last opportunity for a meal for the remainder of the day.

Alaina and Rose had counted on that as they had laid out their plan. In fact, everything depended on getting the Englishman and the money off the train, even if only for a moment. Pretending to be disinterested, Alaina reached into her bag and retrieved a book which she began to read.

The Englishman immediately seized upon the opportunity to strike up a conversation again. "I say, Miss, uh..." he paused, as if waiting for her to offer her name. When she failed to respond, he continued, "Might I ask the nature of your literary material?"

Alaina looked over the top of the book briefly and then answered as she pretended to return her attention to the pages. "The title is *Grey Rocks: A Tale of the Middle West* by Willis George Emerson. Mr. Emerson is a novelist from right here in Wyoming, and not only a novelist, but quite an accomplished orator and political spokesman, as well."

"And how is it, may I ask, that a young lady such as yourself has managed to become so cultivated and proficient in scholarly achievement?"

Alaina lowered the book and replied, "My mother is an attorney and insisted that her children not grow up illiterate, even though we are forced to exist in this god-forsaken wasteland." The last statement was in response to the gentleman's earlier description of her homeland.

"I do beg your pardon!" the young Englishman stammered. "I fear I have been misled to believe that the inhabitants of the northwestern country were an uneducated lot. I realize my vast misconception and solicit your forgiveness."

Alaina hid her slight smile behind the book and peering again over the top, she replied, "Quite all right, Sir. Not everyone out here has been afforded the same privilege for education as I. Nevertheless, I believe you will find that what they lack in formal tutorage, they tend to make up for with common sense and ingenuity."

She could scarcely refrain from bursting out with laughter. She almost felt sorry for the poor man, but it was a part of her strategy to place him on the defense and cause him a little embarrassment to be used to her advantage later. Still, she regretted having to put him in his place so ruthlessly.

The Englishman turned his attention to the Pinkerton man beside him and began making small talk about their itinerary and estimated time of arrival at their destination. Alaina lifted the book enough to conceal her eyes from the two men and glanced sidelong out the window of the coach to try to recognize the landscape.

Alaina was aware, even before the whistle sounded and the train began to slow, that they were nearing Medicine Bow. She became tense with anticipation as she reached for her bag and prepared to exit the Pullman ahead of the crowd. She glanced toward the hitch rail along the platform of the depot and breathed a sigh of relief upon recognizing her horse and buggy perfectly positioned for her use in the next part of the plan.

She had moved to the door before the train came to a stop, and when the porter pulled it open, she rushed for the buggy. She was seated and ready by the time the four men exited the Pullman and moved toward the hotel across the street. When they reached the center of the broad street, gunshots suddenly rang out from farther down the boardwalk and from the alleyway along the hotel.

Alaina saw her opportunity as the young Englishman turned back toward the safety of the train. She ran her buggy between him and the train and yelled excitedly. "Get in." The man hesitated. "Get in the buggy," she screamed at the top of her voice, "They're after you and that bag." He leaped into the buggy, and Alaina slapped the gelding on the rump with the reins and yelled, "Hiyaah."

They raced down main street in a cloud of dust while gunshots continued to pierce the air from both ends of town. Alaina looked back to see the Pinkerton men scrambling for cover as bullets kicked up dust all around them. She reined the gelding onto the narrow road that ran from Medicine Bow toward Wells Flats to the north—and her father's ranch.

Alaina purposely kept the gelding in a hard run for the first three miles out of town. John Christopher was kept busy just trying to keep from being thrown from the buggy. As the road crested over a sandstone knoll, she swung the buggy to the right off the road along the sandstone ridge and into a large grove of pines. She continued deep into the woods until she came to a depression much like a bowl, and as she dropped over the rim, she saw what she was looking for.

"Hola, Muchacho," she shouted as she pulled hard on the reins, bringing the buggy to a stop.

"Hola," Rose responded. She stood holding Badger and Amiga with the spare saddle lying at her feet.

"Hurry," Alaina continued. "We have to move fast."

She moved to the gelding and slid the harness to the ground. Rose was at her side with the saddle and bridle already placing the bit in his mouth as Alaina swung the saddle over and quickly pulled the cinch strap tight. They turned to see the Englishman staring at them in bewilderment. Taking the queue, Alaina spoke first.

"Mr. Braunche, I know you must have a lot of questions, but now is not the time. You must trust us. We are not after your money, but someone is. We are going to do everything in our power to see that you deliver it to the proper recipients. In order to do that, we have to keep you off of that train and out of sight until I can find my father and Sheriff Frost. Now, will you cooperate?"

"I would be most happy to cooperate if you would be so kind as to explain to me one detail. If you are attempting to assist me, then why were those men back there trying to kill me?"

Alaina chuckled, "That was nothing but a diversion to get you away from the Pinkertons. Rose paid a few young ranch hands with a five-dollar gold piece to each of them to scare the pants off of an English greenhorn… you Mr. Braunche. They were shooting into the dirt. Otherwise you and those Pinkertons would be lying dead in the street back there. Now, can you ride?" Alaina asked.

The Englishman nodded.

"Let's go then. Keep in between Rose and me. Oh, by the way, Anarosa, meet John Christopher Braunche from London, England. John Christopher, Rose." With that she quickly moved to Badger's side and stepped into the saddle.

The three riders pushed their mounts hard through the early afternoon. Alaina led them through the foothills along the edge of the pines, being careful not to silhouette themselves against the skyline. She looked over her shoulder from time to time, checking on their English friend. She was pleasantly surprised at his horsemanship. He was obviously a skilled rider, although a little clumsy with the western saddle. After a few hours of hard riding, they came upon a small stream winding through some large boulders and tall Ponderosa Pines. Alaina pulled up and dismounted.

"Let's give the horses a breather. I think we have put enough space between ourselves and anyone who might be looking for our trail. It would have taken them a while to locate the carriage. We can make it to my father's line shack before dark." She looked at John Christopher as she spoke. "Rose and I will tell you the whole story when we get there. Once you hear everything we have to say, and hear what was waiting for you fifty miles on down the track, I believe you will be more than ready to trust that we have your best interest at heart.

Oh, and I apologize for having had to deceive you on the train, but it was necessary in order to get you out of harm's way. Now, if you will excuse me, I need to change my attire. This evening gown is not designed for western saddlery." With that, she reached for her bag that she had hooked over her saddle horn and picked her way carefully through the rocks to a secluded spot among the boulders.

When Alaina returned, she was dressed in a western-style riding habit she had designed herself. The upper body was cut like a fashionable lady's dress with a wasp-like waist, but the skirt was split to allow riding astride rather than side-saddle. She had exchanged the high-top lace up shoes for her western riding boots. She noticed John Christopher's gaze follow her as she approached.

A pleasing smile curled her lips as she broke the silence. "Mr. Braunche, if you will kindly put your eyes back inside their sockets and mount up, we will be off." She was sure that his face turned a light shade of red as he began to stammer.

"Oh, I beg your pardon, Miss…uh, by the way, Miss, I never caught your name. You were kind enough to introduce me to Miss Rose, but as of yet, you've failed to give me *your* name."

"Alaina…my name is Alaina Marie Johnson. My father is a rancher—a horse-breeder with a fairly large spread a little north of here. That is where we are heading at the present time. Sheriff Marc Frost is a long-time family friend, and he'll know what to do about you."

"Alaina Marie," he spoke her name almost reverently. "I do believe that is the perfect name for you, my dear, and as beautiful as its subject, as ravishing in this wilderness surrounding as you were back there in that luxurious locomotive car."

"I am not 'your dear,' Mr. Braunche," Alaina almost snapped. "And you must keep your mind on the business at hand. I do not think you realize how precarious your life is at the present."

"As I was saying, Miss Alaina Marie," the Englishman broke in, "I beg your pardon if I seemed to be staring. I mean no disrespect. I simply am aghast at the misrepresentation I have been given concerning the female gender upon the western frontier. I am of the opinion that both you and Miss Rose leave the ladies I'm acquainted with in the fair cities of London and Paris far in the shadows with your beauty."

Alaina felt her own cheeks flush with embarrassment but managed to keep her composure as she replied, "Well, Mr. Braunche, I, on the other hand, have been adequately informed concerning you Englishmen. I was under the impression that, as a rule, you talk too much." She smiled as she reached for her stirrup and gained her seat. "Let's make tracks," she shot back over her shoulder as she pointed Badger toward the north and urged him into a gentle canter.

Alaina discovered the small stream she had been looking for a little before sundown. She purposely turned downstream until she came to an area along the stream that was covered with solid granite rock. When all three horses had moved onto the rock surface, she eased Badger into the stream and headed back in the direction they had just come.

"Keep your horses in the water. We don't want company tonight," she said as she continued upstream.

They moved slowly now, allowing the horses to cool, as well as find their footing in the shallow but swift running water. They continued upstream to where a smaller tributary emptied into the one they were following. Alaina turned into the smaller stream as she cautioned the other two about leaving any sign behind.

She was thankful now for all the times her father had instructed her in covering a trail, another talent he had acquired during his life with the Shoshone. She had thought at the time that she was just appeasing him by pretending it was something she would ever need to know. After about half an hour, the smaller stream opened into a clearing that was surrounded by huge boulders and tall Ponderosa pines. A small log cabin was nestled among the Ponderosas a few hundred feet from the water's edge.

The old cabin had been built by her father when he first arrived back in the area after being held captive by Indians as a boy. In recent years, it had been used as a line shack for temporary housing during roundups and what have you. Alaina knew it was fully equipped with staple supplies and cooking utensils.

She rode to the little barn and began unsaddling Badger. The others followed suit, and they soon released the horses into the paddock next to the barn and placed the saddles and gear in the tack room. Alaina pulled the latch string that hung on the outside of the cabin door and pushed the door wide open to allow enough light to find the kerosene lantern and matches. In a matter of minutes, she had a warm fire crackling in the small fireplace. She reached above the mantle for the little cane pole that had rested there since her first memory of the place.

"I'll be back shortly," she said as she slipped out the door, closing it behind her.

Moving to the edge of the stream, she turned over a flat rock that was half buried in the rich soil and gathered up half a dozen wiggling red worms. Threading one onto the fishhook, she dropped it into the stream below a large rock where the water formed a little eddy. Immediately the line became taught, and she hauled in a large brook trout from the swirling water. Repeating the process several times provided an ample number of the speckled delicacies for a good meal. She cleaned them quickly, washing them in the stream and made her way back through the twilight to the cabin.

John Christopher had sat quietly watching the two girls prepare the meal and then became completely involved in devouring his man's share of the delicious brook trout, along with the fried potatoes and cornbread. He finally pushed away from the small table and leaned against the back of his chair with a look of complete satisfaction on his face.

"Ladies," he broke the silence at last, "I must say that I have never enjoyed such extraordinary culinary skill in all of my life. Who would believe that such a fine feast is just lying here miles from the nearest restaurateur, waiting for the simple sizzling skillet to bring out the wondrous flavor therein?"

The two girls looked at one another and smiled. Rose responded, "Señor Braunche, you speak many words to flatter, but *gracias, Señor*, from each of us."

They then began to tell their entire story, beginning with Alaina's departure for San Francisco on the train. They revealed every part of their adventure while the Englishman sat transfixed in his chair.

When the girls finally fell silent, John Christopher responded.

"I have come to fully understand the peril that awaited me only a few miles farther on my journey. I cannot adequately express my gratitude to you both, but I can assure you that you have my full cooperation from this moment forth. Were I in my own environment, I would have an inkling how to proceed, but I am afraid I must rely completely on your intuition, and I must say, based on your performance thus far, I feel that I am in adequate hands. However, I must inform you that you will be up against the best that the Pinkerton Agency has to offer, and I am certain, considering the amount of money that they were entrusted to protect, there will be dozens more on the way."

"Then we will have to act fast," Alaina began. "That will not be our only concern. The men who were waiting at Walcott Junction to relieve you of that money will be fit to be tied when they discover that someone beat them to the punch. As you know by Rose's former experience with the leader of that gang, they will be ruthless in their effort to get their hands on that bag. I know it's asking a lot, but I think you should stash it somewhere until we can assure its safe delivery to Encampment."

"I cannot, in good conscience, allow myself that luxury," he replied. "I have been entrusted with the task of delivering it into the hands of the chairman of the board of directors at the smelter plant in Encampment. I have given my word, and my word is my bond. I will carry out my assignment or die in the process."

"Well, I admire your character," Alaina responded. "As long as you know that it may very well come to that…your life, I mean. We will get some rest and come daylight I will ride to Wells Flats and locate Sheriff

Frost. Then I will go to the ranch and enlist my father. He will know what to do."

Alaina gathered bedrolls from the tack room, and she and Rose allowed John Christopher the bunk. He reached into his coat pocket for the key to the handcuffs and unlocked the restraint around his wrist. After rubbing the circulation back for a moment, he handed the bag to Alaina.

"I am fully aware that, were it not for you, this would now be out of my hands. I would be obliged if you would place it somewhere out of sight until we are ready to continue on our journey."

Alaina took the bag and climbed the ladder to the small attic space above the bunk and shoved it back into the darkest corner. "I'm afraid that is the best I can do for now. If anyone gets to that bag they will have to go over you first." Alaina went to the door and pulled the latch string through the hole from outside the door, then fitted the bar in the brackets to secure it from the inside.

13. Home is Where the Heart Is

The early spring morning showed great promise of an early thaw. The sun was already warming the tiny glen in the upper foothills as Alaina saddled Badger. A new excitement stirred her today. She had been away for almost three months, the longest period she had ever been separated from her parents and the ranch in one stretch.

It felt comfortable and satisfying just to be back in familiar surroundings after the harrowing experience she had been through, but there was a longing within to see her mother and father. She wondered if her mother had finished with the court case in San Francisco by now and hoped that she had. Rose and John Christopher bid her goodbye as she reached for the stirrup.

"I should be back by noon," she informed them. "However, if I have a problem locating Sheriff Frost, it could be later. I plan to go by the ranch house and bring my father back with me. You two need to stay out of site in case those Pinkerton agents are better trackers than I credit them to be."

Both the Englishman and the young Mexican girl nodded in agreement as she whirled Badger and nudged him into a quick canter along the trail to Wells Flats. The morning sky was clear blue, the snow had begun to melt away on the south facing slopes, and tiny sprigs of green grass already showed in some areas where the sun warmed the bare earth. Small herds of antelope drifted into higher elevations searching for new areas for grazing.

Alaina felt a peace about her that she hadn't experienced for a long while. She recognized it as the feeling one gets when you are home.

She had been in the saddle for less than an hour when the trail that wound through the foothills from the line shack intercepted the road that reached from Medicine Bow to the little village of Wells Flats. Alaina hoped to find Sheriff Frost there or at least learn where he was today. The territory of his jurisdiction was vast, and he made it a point to show his presence periodically at different locations so that folks would know he was on the job.

No sooner had she turned toward the village when the road climbed up and over a saddle in the hills. As she reached the top where she could see the downhill side, she noticed two horsemen ridding side by side less than a mile ahead. She pulled Badger up abruptly and instinctively reached for the binoculars in her saddle bag, wondering if these could be two of the Pinkerton agents scouring the country for the Englishman.

As she lifted the binoculars to her eyes and focused in on the two riders, however, she began to smile. Placing the binoculars back in their place, she pulled the saddle gun from its scabbard and jacked a cartridge into the chamber. Two consecutive shots pierced the morning silence as Alaina levered the rifle and squeezed the trigger in quick succession, then after a short pause, a third round.

She need not wonder if her father and Sheriff Frost heeded the signal. She knew without a doubt that they would immediately rein their horses to a stop and look in her direction. It was a signal she and her father had agreed upon years ago when she had first been allowed to carry a rifle. She nudged Badger into a fast canter and within a few minutes joined the two men who were standing beside their horses waiting to welcome her home.

"Daughter, where have you been, and what have you been up to?" Tall yelled, before she had even reached them. She lit off of Badger before he came to a full stop and ran into her father's arms. After squeezing him for a long minute, she turned to Marc and repeated the greeting. There was so much to tell, and she had no idea how to begin.

"Dad," she blurted breathlessly, "I need your advice and your help… and yours, too, Uncle Marc." Sheriff Frost wasn't really related, but she had called him Uncle all of her life. "I'll tell you the whole story as we go along, but we need to get back to the line shack as quickly as possible."

"Hold on there, young lady. You are not going anywhere else until you set your mother's mind at ease. Do you have any conception of the mental anguish you have caused the both of us!" Tall raged in an upbraiding tone.

"Yes, Daddy," she began, using the term of endearment as a cushion from his displeasure. "I surely do understand, but after you hear everything, you will agree that I had no choice."

"Well, whatever it is that you have going at the line shack will have to wait until we go to the ranch and visit your mother. But first we will stop at 'the Flats' up here and see if she is there even now, checking for any word from you or me."

"I haven't seen her myself since she returned from California. Thanks to you, I've been chasing all over two states, sleeping on the cold ground and living on jerky and hard tack." His last statement was designed to cause at least a little bit of remorse on Alaina's part as payback for the worry and anxiety she had brought on everyone. Alaina gave him a sheepish sidewise glance in response.

A quick visit to the Union Pacific office told them that Cat had been there that morning but had already returned to the ranch. They remounted and pushed the horses into a long canter. Tall and the sheriff could each sense the urgency in Alaina's manner and resolved to escort her back to the line shack immediately after a short visit to the ranch.

* * *

Alana's mother had struggled for the past several weeks with the question of where her place should be. She had made the long journey back from San Francisco, knowing she had to find her child, only to be confronted on her arrival at the ranch with the dilemma of how best to go about that. She wanted to be out there with her husband in the search, but she also realized the importance of someone maintaining a presence at home in case Alaina showed up there.

She had made at least one trip each day to the Union Pacific office ten miles away hoping to hear from either Tall or Alaina. The days had crawled by at a snail's pace with hardly a word, and often when word came from Tall it was to inquire if Alaina had come home, not to inform her that Alaina had been found. The pain of not knowing what was going on had become unbearable at times.

The news had finally come that Alaina had been seen in Rawlins. That was a hundred miles away but some consolation, at least, but the question still paramount in Cat's mind was, why all of this mystery? Why was her little girl traipsing all over the state of Wyoming rather than coming straight home? Something was amiss for sure, and Cat was beside herself. Even the latest word she had received, that Alaina was in Laramie and that she would be home in a few days, was very mysterious in nature. Cat knew down deep that there was a great deal more to the story, and she had to know what Alaina was up to. Her concern was not out of distrust, but rather her motherly instinct to protect her child.

She had stood in front of the large window in the parlor looking down the lane that led toward the main road, wrestling with the urge to saddle up and head toward Laramie. Then the disturbing thought returned. What if word came that Alaina had turned up somewhere else, even here at the ranch?

She sighed heavily, coming to a decision. At least she could ride back to Wells Flats and check at the telegraph office for any news even though she had been there only a few hours ago.

She was about to fetch her coat and hat when a movement caught her eye down the lane. She stopped and turned her full attention to the window and immediately recognized Tall rounding the curve in the road. Then another rider showed, and then a third. Her heart leapt into her throat as she realized without a doubt that the third horse and rider was Badger and her missing child.

She lost all sense of time and distance; her only interest at this moment was her husband and the young girl on horseback coming up the lane. Her next realization was that of holding her daughter close to her, caressing her, scolding her, squeezing her, and covering her with tears of joy.

"Mom, I'm okay," Alaina insisted, finally warding off the lavish attention. "I had no choice but to do what I could to help Rose. You'll get to meet Rose; she is the sweetest thing. As far the other thing, I couldn't think of any other way to keep people safe and keep the money from being lost."

Alaina had the full attention of all three in her audience now. Bombarded with questions coming all at once, she finally held up her hands in desperation.

"Okay, I understand that you have to know the full story…but can't we be riding while we talk? There is still much to be done, and I am not sure how to go about it. Rose and John Christopher are hidden away at the line shack and are still in grave danger of being discovered.

"If the Pinkerton men find them, they will treat Rose badly and take John Christopher with them. They will walk right into an ambush waiting for them at Walcott Junction. If that gang from Utah somehow found out they were outsmarted, they will be after the money, and they will stop at nothing, and I mean nothing, to get it."

All three of her listeners stood speechless now, realizing that what Alaina had been involved in while she was away was not a young girl's frivolous adventure but rather something profoundly serious. Cat greeted her husband whom she had not seen since her departure for San Francisco several months previous. Then she and Marc greeted one another, in turn. They then all agreed that they should hurry back to the line shack.

Cat quickly gathered up a few articles in case it became necessary for her to be away for a while. They rode at a brisk walk for the first several minutes while Alaina briefly gave the highlights of her experience, adding that she would fill in the blanks when Rose and John Christopher were present to also tell their story.

Nudging their mounts into a long canter, they quickly covered the fifteen-mile distance to the mountain hideaway. Alaina breathed a sigh of relief to discover everything just as she left it that morning.

The four newcomers unsaddled their mounts and turned them into the paddock where they immediately rolled in the snow. After a round of sniffing and squealing between them and the other horses, they began searching the premises for fresh sprigs of green grass.

Rose and John Christopher dared not show themselves outside the cabin, realizing that they could very well be under surveillance from any number of high vantage points in the rocks and boulders along the mountainside to the north. During Alaina's absence, Rose had described to John Christopher in her best broken English how the man who was after the bag of investment money had shot his partner in crime in cold blood. He then had brutally beaten her and had beaten her brother to death. She told him about the tender care she had received from Alaina over a period of several weeks, without which she would not be alive to be speaking with him today.

As he listened again to the entire episode involving Alaina's heroic performance throughout the process of events that had brought them all together, he had developed an admiration for the young Wyoming frontier girl like he had never held toward anyone, let alone a woman. He found it difficult to believe that anyone Alaina's age could have the courage or the clever ingenuity to contrive and instigate the plan to remove both himself and the huge sum of investment money from the hands of three of the best Pinkerton agents available. He came to fully realize that, above all, he also owed her his life and would be forever indebted to her for that alone.

He and Rose had been watching the four new arrivals through the small glass paned windows in the front of the cabin and readily pulled the door open for them to enter with their gear. Immediately Alaina began introductions.

"This is Anarosa," she began. "I call her Rose, and this is John Christopher Braunche from London, England, and the representative for eastern and foreign investors in the smelter plant in Encampment." As she pointed to each one, in turn, she introduced her mother, her father, and Sheriff Marc Frost, whom she referred to as Uncle Marc.

"The first requisite is for everyone to understand the full magnitude of what is at stake. That will require a complete recap of everything that has happened up until now. Then we have to decide a course of action from this point forth."

She went to the ladder and retrieved the large bag of money from the tiny attic above, then the six inhabitants of the small cabin each found a place to sit while Alaina and Rose once again told their story. When it came to the part involving John Christopher, he was more than happy to include his embellishing account of the remarkable performance of the two young ladies in removing him from the hands of the Pinkerton agents and rescuing him from certain foul play and possibly even death.

Throughout the narrative, Tall and Marc occasionally remarked about how closely entwined their paths had been during the past two months of their search for Alaina. After several minutes of questions and discussion, Sheriff Frost made the first contribution for a plan of action.

"Well, first, the Pinkerton Agency has to be informed that their client is safe, as well as the cargo that is in his trust. As for the gang waiting to intercept the money, we need to not only prevent that from happening but also apprehend them for the crimes already committed."

He turned to speak directly to his comrade, "Tall, I will deputize you, and you and I will take John Christopher here and incorporate the help of the Pinkertons. Together we should be able to outfox that gang that is waiting for the money to arrive on a train. The girls can go back to the ranch with Cat. They should be safe there."

Alaina had never in her life talked back to her Uncle Marc, but his intention to cut her and Rose out of the equation quickly caused her blood to boil. She spoke before even considering the consequence. "Rose and I haven't come this far and risked our lives to save this bag of money from falling into the wrong hands just to turn tail and run like cowards. That man tried to kill Rose and intended to kill us both. We owe him," Alaina blurted.

"All the more reason for you to stay out of it now that it is in the hands of the law," Tall scolded, but he forced himself to take control of his emotions. "I can't express how proud I am of you. Your presence of mind thus far is beyond my wildest expectation, but you must realize that from here on the stakes are much higher. Up until now, you and Rose have been a minor obstacle to that murdering outlaw who is after this money, but after what you have been able to accomplish to stop him, you are now a major threat as well as a bitter enemy.

"He will stop at nothing to rid himself of you, and I will not allow you to put your life in jeopardy needlessly. You go back to the ranch with your mother and let the sheriff handle it from here on. I'll be glad to do what I can to help him."

"Yes, Alaina," Cat agreed. "I couldn't bear another day of wondering if you are safe or not. You and Rose have done more than anyone could expect from you, both of you. Let the men take it from here."

"I have to agree," John Christopher interjected. "I am beholden beyond measure to the both of you, but I must insist that you refrain from placing yourselves at further risk of peril on my behalf. However, I would consider it a great honor to have your consent to call on the two of you at a later date when this entire business is concluded and everyone is safe.

"As a small token of my appreciation, it would be my honor to escort the two of you to an evening on the town, the finest dining and dancing the world has to offer. Money is no object. It would be in the city of your choice and at no expense to you or your family, providing of course that your mother and father could join us. We must keep it all prim and proper."

Alaina looked at Rose in exasperated defeat, completely dismissing the gracious offer from John Christopher. Her mind was completely engrossed with the situation at hand. Anyway, what right did he have to tell her what to do? But how could she dare defy them all?

Rose returned the look with an air of slight vexation and simply shrugged as if she understood. No one waited for either of them to respond but simply began planning their next move. The matter was settled so far as they were concerned. Tall, John Christopher, and Sheriff Frost would ride back to Wells Flats this evening, contact the Pinkerton Agency by telegram and spend the night there. Tomorrow they would do their best to smuggle Mr. Braunche and the money into Encampment. Once the money had safely reached its destination, they would then attempt to apprehend the outlaw gang.

14. Partners

Cat, Alaina, and Rose said their goodbyes to the men and rode north toward the ranch while Tall, John Christopher, and Sheriff Frost rode southeast toward Wells Flats. The women rode in silence while easing their mounts into a slow canter in order to reach the ranch before nightfall. Alaina brooded over the sudden turn of events that had taken her completely off guard.

One minute she was involved in the most exciting adventure of her entire lifetime—passionate about preventing a malicious encroachment upon the life and liberty of other human beings—and the next minute she was being told to go home and basically sit down and shut up.

She wanted to scream and stamp her foot in disgust and humiliation, and would have, had she thought it would help. Instead, she rode in silence allowing her mother to lead the way with Rose following while she lagged to the rear.

Upon arrival at the ranch house, they unsaddled and tended the horses then went directly to the kitchen where Cat began to lay a fire in the big cook stove. Finally, Alaina could stand it no longer.

"How can you do that!" she exclaimed. "How can you just sit here at home, knowing what could happen out there? There are only two of them against God only knows how many in that gang from Utah, and I don't think John Christopher will be of any assistance to Dad and Uncle Marc if it comes to a showdown."

"Alaina," Cat began, "I do not intend to "just sit here," as you so vehemently described it. There is one thing that you need to learn about men right now if you intend to get along in this *man's world*. You can spend your time and energy arguing and trying to buck the system, or you can work with the system.

"First of all, you have to be willing to allow men the gratification of feeling that they are in control. They need that in order to fulfill their role in society. It's how God made them. The woman, on the other hand, God made to be a partner to him. That does not mean to be under him or behind him, but beside him as a partner. That is what we are going to be. We are going to be partners."

Cat allowed herself the pleasure of a secret smile, remembering all the times she'd 'helped' her hardheaded husband. "Now, let's get something prepared to eat, get a good night's sleep, and tomorrow we will decide what these three partners can do to help out in a very dangerous situation."

Seeing the fire light her daughter's eyes, she cautioned, "But, with that in mind, the two of you must promise that you will allow me to decide what we will and will not do in order to help. We will have to use the utmost caution. If any harm were to come to either of you I could never forgive myself."

Alaina suddenly broke into a smile and then a chuckle. *You sly fox you,* she thought to herself. She had just acquired a new appreciation and admiration for her mother. She had imparted that bit of wisdom without the slightest bit of resentment or hostility toward the opposite sex, just stating it as fact in a non-condescending fashion.

Alaina now realized that her mother had never intended to just walk away from the matter. Instead, she separated the three of them from the men to be of greater assistance. This relieved the men of the burden of concern for the safety of the women, allowing them to concentrate fully on the business at hand.

* * *

Cat, Alaina, and Rose sat at breakfast the following morning discussing the combination of circumstances that brought them all together. Rose was given unequivocal assurance from both Cat and Alaina that her place would always be with them. She was to consider herself to be family. Tears welled in her eyes as she thanked them both for their kindness.

"I want a sister all my life," she said in broken English as she smiled at Alaina.

"Me, too," Alaina replied as she patted Rose's hand.

"Now, what are we going to do about this situation with the boys?" Cat questioned. "They will be on their way to Medicine Bow by now. I am thinking that we should saddle up and follow along at a distance in case they need us. If we are careful, they will not suspect that we are anywhere but here at the ranch. I'm not completely convinced that the solution to all of this is as simple as Sheriff Frost seems to think."

The two girls expressed their complete agreement and immediately set about cleaning the kitchen. Afterwards, all three began packing for a possible extended stay away from home. Alaina showed Rose her closet and suggested she pick out several items of clothing that suited her until she could purchase new ones for herself.

Following her own advice, she threw together a travel bag to carry her through at least a week. As an afterthought, she reached for the gun and holster that hung on a nail inside the closet door. It was a Colt 45 her father had given her years before. He had said it was for protection while out on the range. One never knew what danger might be lurking in the dark woods and Rocky Mountain Crags where she spent much of her time.

She had needed to use it on a few occasions to scare off mountain lions and bears. When she rode alone, it was always strapped around her waist for quick and easy reach, but she didn't know why she felt the need to have it with her on this trip. Considering all she and Rose had been through, it just seemed like the thing to do. She stuffed it into her bulging bag and fastened the flap. As they saddled up at the tack shed, she reached for her lariat and fastened it to her saddle horn with the leather latigo that always hung there. She never intended to go anywhere again without a rope.

* * *

Sheriff Frost led the way down the main street of Medicine Bow, scouring the boardwalks and streets ahead for any sign of danger. He had been in tight spots before, and knew that the best way for a man to save his own hide was to keep out of those situations. His first interest was to locate the Pinkerton agents.

He had telegraphed Pinkerton headquarters in Chicago the evening before and let them know that he was in possession of both the emissary and the large amount of investment money destined for Encampment, Wyoming, and would be arriving in Medicine Bow around noon the following day. He half expected to be intercepted at the edge of town, but so far no one had showed. They traveled the length of the main street three abreast with John Christopher in the middle between himself and Tall. When they reached the jail where Sheriff Frost had a circuit office, they dismounted and quickly crossed the boardwalk and hurried through the doorway.

Marc was the first to enter, and so the first to find himself looking across his own desk into the face of a man he had never seen before. As his eyes adjusted to the semi-darkness, he realized that several other men stood against the walls of the room with pistols drawn, trained on the three who had just entered.

"Mr. Frost, I presume," were the first words spoken by the man behind the desk. "I am Agent Abernathy of the Pinkerton National Detective Agency. I am also an appointed Deputy United States Marshal. I have been instructed to place both you and your deputy here under arrest for interference in matters pertaining to the office of the United States Marshal. So, if you will…kindly lift your hands away from your gun belts."

Marc and Tall had both sized up the situation as the man spoke, and each one realized there was no chance to turn the tables on so many guns. They lifted their hands slowly and felt the weight of their side arms being removed from their holsters. Marc swore under his breath. This was the second time in as many months he had allowed himself to be relieved of his side arm. That was more than he could remember in his entire life. "I'm getting too old for this," he muttered to himself.

"Agent Abernathy, there is really no need for this," he began. "As you can see, I am an officer of the law myself, and we are here to assure that Mr. Braunche and the investment money he is transporting arrive safely to their destination."

"Sheriff Frost," Abernathy responded, "That is precisely what I and my men were in the process of doing when you interfered. Now, would you mind stepping into that empty cell, please?"

The instant Abernathy finished speaking, both Marc and Tall were shoved through the door of the adjoining cell. They turned back facing

120

their opponents only to find the cell door slamming shut before them. For the first time, they were able to fully access their circumstances. The small room in the front part of the jail was crowded with men wearing badges. Two of them wore shields identical to the one on Abernathy's jacket lapel. A large cocky sort of man wore a sheriff's star, and five other men wore deputy sheriff badges.

I haven't seen this much law in this state in all my life, Tall thought. He was about to open his mouth to speak when John Christopher beat him to it.

"Agent Abernathy, I believe I can satisfy any misunderstanding as pertaining to these two gentlemen." Before he could carry it any further, he was cut short.

"Mr. Braunche, I am sure you mean well, but you and the money that has been placed in your charge are actually my responsibility. It is my job to deliver both you and it to Encampment, Wyoming, and I intend to do that because my job depends on it. Once that is accomplished, we will sort out the rest of this.

"The truth as far as I see it is, me and my men were fired upon, and you were unlawfully taken out of our hands. My orders were clear, and I have followed them. Now, we are already two days behind schedule. I suggest you cooperate fully and place yourself into my care voluntarily, or else I shall have to use force. Do you understand?"

"I have reason to believe that these men with you are hoodlums disguised as law officers, Sir." John Christopher blurted.

"You can believe anything you like." Abernathy snarled. "This sheriff and his men were hired by the stage line that will take us from Walcott Junction to Encampment. I very well doubt that the stage line would engage the services of anyone with whom they were not fully confident. Now, what is it going to be Mr. Braunche? Are you coming peacefully, or do you wear my cuffs along with the pair that has you fastened to that bag of money? Makes no difference with me. The afternoon train will be rolling in any minute, and you're going to be on it."

"Abernathy, you're making a grave mistake." Sheriff Frost protested, but to no avail. The room emptied except for one of the Pinkerton agents who was left to watch over the prisoners. A train whistle sounded in the distance signaling the arrival of the afternoon train. Marc and Tall looked at one another shaking their heads in disbelief of what had just happened.

"Mr....whatever your name is," Sheriff Frost began. "You've got to believe us. Your boss and Mr. Branuche are walking right into a trap. They will likely be killed, and the money will be lost. You need to let us out of here so we can stop it."

The Pinkerton man smiled wryly. He chuckled softly as he began to speak. "I've read all of the dime novels about the wild, wild west, Sheriff. I would bet that you two imagine yourselves to be like the characters in those dime novels, bound by your moral conscience to save the world from the bad men. Just so you know, I wasn't born yesterday, and the wild, wild west is long gone. So, you two may as well sit yourselves down and relax. You're going to be here for a while."

Realizing that any attempt to reason with this man would be futile, Marc and Tall went to the small window in the back of the cell and watched as the train began its departure, rolling slowly past their window, picking up steam as it rounded the bend going out of town.

* * *

The distant scream of a train whistle pierced the tranquil Wyoming afternoon as three women approached the little western town of Medicine Bow. They had purposely not been in a hurry. The plan was to remain unnoticed by the three men they were trailing. They really had no idea what to expect, and so they slowed their mounts to a brisk walk as they neared the first buildings along main street.

Cat suggested that Alaina and Rose fall behind several paces so as not to draw attention. One or two riders usually were not noticed too much riding into a town, but three or more riding in together seemed to always turn all eyes of curiosity their way. Cat looked down the street toward the Sheriff's Office at the far end of town, searching for the three mounts the men were riding. To her surprise, there were no horses tied to the hitch rail, but there were three being led up the street toward them by a man she thought she recognized as the livery stable attendant.

Although she was still a quarter of a mile away, there was no doubt in her mind about their identity. She would pick Sassy and Hermes out of a whole corral full of horses. She motioned for Alaina and Rose to stay behind as she nudged her gelding into a long canter. Cat was well acquainted with the livery attendant. She often left her horse in his care when catching a train to one of the many distant cities where duty called her these days.

"Eli," she called while still several yards away, "Can you tell me where Tall and Sheriff Frost are?"

"Yes Ma'am, I surely can," the young man replied with widening eyes. "They have been locked up in jail. I ain't never heered of a sheriff being locked up in his own jail. What's goin' on, Mrs. Johnson?"

"Well, I don't know, Eli. Suppose you tell me everything you know about it."

"Well, all I know is I was sent a message to come and get these horses and take care of them until the sheriff and Mr. Johnson was let out of jail."

"Okay, Eli, thanks. I think you should just loosen the girths and leave the saddles on them for now. Give them a good portion of grain and hay. We'll be calling for them in a few hours."

"Yes, Mrs. Johnson. I'll take good care of them for you. I know the sheriff and Mr. Johnson ain't done nothin' to break the law. This is all mighty strange if ye ask me."

Cat whirled her mount sharply around and gave him a firm nudge with her heels. She was back to Alaina and Rose in a short minute. "Looks like our plan to stay in the shadows has been foiled. Your father and the Sheriff are locked in jail. We had better go see what the situation is."

They traveled the quarter of a mile back to the jail together without worry of drawing attention now. Alaina followed her mother through the door but quickly turned her back to the man behind the desk. She recognized him immediately as one of the Pinkerton agents from her train ride from Laramie a few days before. She noticed her father and Sheriff Frost looking at her questioningly. She placed her finger in front of her lips signaling them to silence. Her mother spoke to the Pinkerton man in a stern tone.

"Why are these men in jail?" she demanded, straight to the point.

"They have been placed under arrest for interference in matters pertaining to the office of the United States Marshal." The man spouted, parroting what he had heard previously from his superior. "My orders are to keep them here until Agent Abernathy returns from Encampment, possibly two days from now, seeing they just left on the afternoon train. At that time, he will correspond with the U.S. Marshal's office for further instructions about proceeding with prosecution for the crimes committed."

Alaina moved to the door of the cell and being careful to keep her mother between herself and the man behind the desk, she motioned to her father and Sheriff Frost to come closer. She reached through the bars and gave each of them a hug, quickly snatching the badges from their vests and placing them inside her coat pocket. She then turned and without a word, slipped through the door and across the boardwalk to where Badger stood.

She stepped into the stirrup and slowly rode back down Main Street until well out of earshot of the jail. She nudged Badger with her heels as she drew air through her lips with a loud kissing signal that called on him for everything he had. He immediately shot forward into full speed, and the two of them left town heading north in a cloud of dust.

Alaina had quickly assessed the situation back at the jail. She visualized John Christopher walking headlong into trouble that might very well claim his life. The only way that could be avoided was to free her father and Sheriff Frost as quickly as possible. Even then, catching up to John Christopher in time might be out of the question. She had formulated a plan that might work, but it required the help of someone that the Pinkerton agent back at the jail would not recognize.

The Rocking "O" Ranch headquarters lay about ten miles north of Medicine Bow. Some of the young cowboys who worked there were the men Rose had hired with a twenty-dollar gold piece to each one, for staging the shootout in Medicine Bow a few days before. Alaina was acquainted with them because of the stock roundups that brought all the ranch hands together every spring. She had been involved with those roundups since she was a toddler.

Every young rider in the country was smitten by the young Alaina Johnson. Alaina knew that, although she was careful not to let it go to her head. She considered them each one to be friends but took great care not to encourage any kind of romantic advance from any of them. She also knew that they would walk through coals of fire for her if she would just ask, but she was prepared to reward them again monetarily for their services in order to avoid feeling otherwise obligated.

Badger kept the pace without letting up until the ranch house came into view. Alaina was relieved to see a group of cowboys gathered around the corral fence as she drew near. A corral full of young horses told her they were in the process of breaking in new mounts for the coming spring roundup.

She headed straight for the men who had assisted Rose a few days ago and wasted no time explaining what was going on. As briefly as possible, she described what she wanted to do and offered two twenty-dollar gold pieces each for two men who would help get her father and Sheriff Frost out of jail. She was careful to make sure they understood that there was danger involved. Two young men stepped forward before she had even finished speaking.

"Sky and me will go with you," the young cowboy volunteered. "You can forget about the money though. If your daddy is in jail, there's something that ain't right."

"Well, there may be consequences," Alaina cautioned again. "If we get caught, you could be prosecuted for participating in a jail break."

Alaina knew the name of the young man who had volunteered only by what the other ranch hands called him. He and the one he called Sky were brothers and had come to Wyoming four or five years back. They had hired on with a trail drive to bring a herd of longhorns up from south Texas. After the herd was sold, they decided they had enough of the rattlesnakes and mesquite brush down south and found work at the Rocking "O".

The cowboys there dubbed them "Tuff" and "Sky" in honor of their tenacity when it came to buckin' out the riding stock. They had both been schooled on the wild Spanish ponies that were brought up to south Texas from Mexico. To hear them tell it, there was not a wilder, meaner, more savage beast walkin' on God's green earth than one of them cussed Spanish mustangs. The local cowboys claimed that Sky could ride a bronc higher than anybody they knew and still come down in the middle. And Tuff… well, the handle speaks for itself. He could take a beatin' like no one else they knew and walk away without a flinch.

"Well then, we'll just have to be sure we don't get caught," Tuff retorted to Alaina, smiling.

"Okay, if you're sure, here is what I need you to do," explained Alaina.

* * *

Less than an hour had passed when the three riders rode back into Medicine Bow. Alaina asked the two cowboys to wait for her at the livery stable. She headed straight for the train depot where the Western Union Office was located. She breathed a sigh of relief when she entered and found the depot empty except for the agent. She quickly explained to him that she needed his help and that lives, and a great deal of money, rested on his being willing to trust her and to do what she asked.

The agent knew Alaina well and knew that she was a close friend to Sheriff Frost. A few minutes later, she left the depot with a telegram in her hand and rejoined her two accomplices at the livery stable. Cat and Rose were waiting there as well. Not knowing what had happened to Alaina when she left the jail so hurriedly, they came back to the livery to stay out of sight until she showed up. Alaina motioned for all of them to follow her into one of the stalls where they would be out of sight and earshot.

She gave the badges and the telegram to Tuff and Sky and explained what they should do. They pinned on the badges and quickly mounted up and rode down the street to the jail. As they stepped up onto the board walk, Tuff folded the telegram and placed it in the inside pocket of his vest and led the way into the jail.

Tall recognized both young cowboys the instant they entered. He also noticed, and recognized, the badges they wore. He gently nudged Sheriff Frost and motioned for him to keep quiet.

The Pinkerton man sat leaning back in his chair with his feet propped up on the desk when Sky and Tuff came through the door. He quickly dragged his feet off onto the floor and sat up straight at the sight of the two lawmen.

"I'm sheriff McKinsey from over in Laramie County," Tuff stated, while reaching inside his vest for the telegram. "My deputy and I have been ordered by the U.S. Marshal's office to transport two men from your custody to be held at the Federal Penitentiary in Laramie until such time as a court date can be set." With that he pushed the telegram across the desk toward the Pinkerton agent.

"I've not been notified of any of this," the agent protested while glancing over the telegram.

"Well, that is because the U.S. Marshal's office didn't want to risk word getting out about what was happening before we could get here for the prisoners. We have practically rode our horses to death because of the urgency they put on the situation. They are afraid that the local folks around here might try to take matters into their own hands and break these two out of jail.

"Now, if you want to contact the marshal's office in Washington then you do what you have to do, but I want it noted that if anything happens to these two while we wait, it's on your head, not ours."

"Well, it all looks authentic enough. I just wish I had a few more people giving me orders. How am I supposed to know which one to listen to?" he complained.

The two young cowboys drew their pistols from their holsters and pointed them toward Tall and Sheriff Frost as the Pinkerton man took a large ring of cell keys from the top drawer of the desk and unlocked the door of the cell. Tuff motioned Tall and Sheriff Frost toward the door with his gun.

As they stepped onto the boardwalk, Eli from the livery stable, came leading Sassy and Hermes. The four men mounted up and Tall and Sheriff Frost led the way up the street going east toward Laramie. Glancing back over his shoulder, Tall watched the Pinkerton agent walk across the street to the saloon.

"Well, we won't have to worry about him for the rest of the day," he said as he smiled to the others.

As they rode past the livery stable, three women rode out the door and headed east, riding along the opposite side of the street from them. When they all reached the end of town, they turned and rode toward the Medicine Bow River. When they reached the cover of the cottonwoods and underbrush along the riverbank, they all pulled up and dismounted.

Tall turned immediately toward Cat and spoke first.

"I don't know how you pulled that off, but Mr. Braunche and Mr. Abernathy will owe you their lives if we can get to Walcott ahead of the stage that arrives from Rawlins. They will have to ride the train to Rawlins and take the stage back from there in the morning. That buys us some time."

"I wish I could take credit, but I had nothing to do with it," Cat replied. "I had no idea what your daughter was up to. You saw her disappear from the jail the same as me. I was waiting for her at the livery stable when these two young men showed up and said she was working on a plan to get the two of you out of jail. She came back with a telegram from the U.S. Marshal's office in Washington, and before I knew what was happening these two were riding off toward the jail.

"Alaina told me what she was up to after they left, but it was a little too late to object at that point. Besides, I am not sure I would have objected. We may all be in more trouble than we can handle when it catches up to us, but right now we need to be riding."

Tuff and Sky removed the badges from their vests and handed them back to Tall and the sheriff, along with the telegram Sky had carefully lifted from the sheriff's desk while the Pinkerton agent was unlocking the cell. Alaina quickly snatched the telegram away, ripped it into pieces, and dropped it into the swirling current of the river.

"We'd like to come along if it's alright," Tuff exclaimed. "Seems like we have a stake in all of this now."

"Well, that may be true," Sheriff Frost broke in, "but you might want to reconsider. Up to this point no one will connect either of you to what has happened. If you go with us now, you may be putting your neck in a noose so to speak."

"Shoot, we ain't had so much fun since we left Texas," Sky chimed in. "Anyway, you may need all of the guns you can get if you get them ole boys cornered."

"That sure is a possibility," the sheriff admitted. "Well, let's mount up. We'll go to Walcott Junction and lay low until the stage shows up in the morning. I figure they will have to ride the train on to Rawlins to secure the money for the night. Then they will either be on the morning train from Rawlins to Walcott and switch over to the stage there or else they will ride the stage from Rawlins to Encampment, and avoid the transfer from train to the stage.

I figure they will ride the train back and catch the stage at Walcott Junction. The Pinkertons will be partial to the security of the train for as long as they can take advantage of it. Either way, I don't expect that bunch of rascals to make their move to steal the money away from the Pinkertons until they get to the hills this side of Encampment. They will have to have someone waiting with horses. I figure right around Jack Creek or Cow Creek and the Sleeping Indian rock outcrop will be the likely spot. They would have plenty of cover in the rocks anywhere along there, and then they could follow one of those creeks up into the mountains and go over the Continental Divide and back toward their hideout at Brown's Hole. That would be the way I would do it, were I in their shoes."

The seven riders reached Walcott Junction in the middle of the night and found refuge in the cabin of the railroad ticket agent there. Sheriff Frost called him Old Jenkins. They were well acquainted, and the sheriff felt no remorse in getting him out of bed at midnight. A short round of questions told them what Sheriff Frost had suspected. The Pinkerton agent had sent a telegram to Rawlins to arrange for the stage driver to meet them back here at Walcott Junction the following morning. They were to ride the eastbound train back to there and then take the stage from there to Encampment.

Old Jenkins' cabin was small and hardly adequate to provide sleeping arrangements, especially for seven guests. Actually, there were eight counting the reverend who had arrived on the evening stage from Laramie. He introduced himself as Reverend Roger Speers and let it be known that he intended to make sure that every man woman and child in the valley around Saratoga, Wyoming heard the gospel news, and if by chance they would give their life to Jesus he would baptize 'em and disciple 'em in the ways of the Good Book.

Alaina fought back a smile as she thought about the audience the Reverend Speers would have on the journey from there to Saratoga, Pinkerton agents and thieves. Then the thought occurred to her, *what if Sheriff Frost was mistaken and the hoodlums made their play before they reached Saratoga?* She realized that if they said anything to alert the Reverend of the possible danger he was about to subject himself to, it would risk spoiling their chances of saving John Christopher Braunche and the money. She decided immediately to leave that decision up to the sheriff and her dad.

Everyone soon found places to sit and lean up against the wall for a doze here and there. The two young cowboys found a place near Alaina and Rose, and in quiet monotones quizzed them about how they had become involved in all of this. The girls filled them in on every detail of their wild adventure.

Eventually everyone grew tired, and the cabin was silent except for the occasional snore from one spot or another around the room. When dawn began to break and daylight poured through the one small window on the east end of the crowded room, first one then another began to stir until everyone was awake.

When Rose opened her eyes, she immediately looked over to where the two young cowboys had been resting. "Where they go?" she asked abruptly.

There was no sign that Sky or Tuff had ever been there.

"Maybe they needed some privacy," Sheriff Frost suggested. "They will probably be back shortly."

Cat questioned the agent about possibilities for breakfast and learned that he had sourdough in a crock jar on the shelf by the washstand. She built a fire in the small stove in the corner and prepared the dough to make pancakes.

"We've got three hours to kill before the train arrives," Cat offered, "we may as well make good use of it." She poured water and sugar into a small pan for sugar syrup and asked Rose to stir it to keep it from scorching while she poured sourdough onto a hot plate and flipped pancakes until there was a large golden-brown stack waiting for the hungry crowd to devour.

Tall had made a circle around the outdoors to try to locate Tuff and Sky. On checking the stable, he found their horses were gone. The young men were the prime subject of conversation during breakfast. Well, them along with Reverend Speers quoting scripture verse and reference one after another concerning the right path to the kingdom of heaven, and making sure that everyone understood that it's all about Jesus, and that life is uncertain at best, and that there was no reason for anyone to miss out on what the Good Lord in heaven had prepared for His saints.

Alaina was sure and certain that if her folks had not brought her up in a Godly home and led her to believe in the Lord Jesus early on, that her encounter with Reverend Speers would have clinched the fact that she would not have gone another step on this journey without making peace with the Almighty. She had never known a preacher so passionate about his calling.

No one came up with even a remote solution concerning the disappearance of Tuff and Sky but as the morning progressed, their attention was better directed toward the task at hand. Soon the ticket agent excused himself to go to the small station along the track in case there were passengers for the morning train. Alaina could not stand it any longer. Her conscience was eating away at her. if anything were to happen to Reverend Speers, she felt it would be on her. After all, she was the reason they were all here.

What if, she thought to herself. *What if a thousand different what ifs. What if I had not been on that train to California? What if I had not ridden back to Coalville to alert the railroad about the accident? What if I had never run into that imposter sheriff? And what if I had not found out about his scheme to steel the money intended for the smelting plant in Encampment? What if I had never met John Christopher Braunche?*

A warm smile came on her face the instant her thoughts turned to him. He was special, that man. She could not imagine not having met him, and she could not imagine letting anything bad happen to him.

Well, she couldn't do anything to alter the situation for John Christopher right now, but the Reverend was a different thing altogether. She realized she would have to act fast for he was about to leave for the train station to meet the stage for Saratoga. A few brisk steps took her to the door where he was about to exit.

"Reverend Speers, could I have a word with you?" she asked.

"Certainly, what can I do for you young lady?" he queried.

"In private," she implied, as she gave a slight nod of her head toward the door.

Reverend Speers opened the door, and she quickly led him around the corner of the cabin out of sight and hearing of the others.

"Listen, I need you to trust me with what I'm about to tell you," she began. "Don't ask me how I know what I'm about to tell you. You will just have to trust me. There are going to be some bad men on the stage from here to Saratoga. Some really 'bad' men. They are thieves. They are murderers. They have killed before and they intend to kill again. I feel that I must tell you this and ask you not to get on that stage. Your life will be in danger, and I feel responsible."

"My dear child," the reverend began. "Do you not realize that my life is not in your hands, and neither is yours, by the way. Our lives are in the hands of almighty God in heaven. He alone knows every path our lives will take, and He alone has decided and knows the number and the end of our days. He has given each of us a purpose and a course we must take on this day. I will not shirk my duty to go where He has called me.

If, by chance, that takes me to meet my Lord Jesus Christ then it will be okay. But now, I must ask you, are you a born again, washed in the blood, redeemed by His grace, heaven bound child of God? Have you given your heart to Christ, and is your soul in His hands?"

Alaina, stared at the reverend with her eyes widening almost in shock. She had never been confronted about her belief concerning religious matters before. She hesitated briefly while collecting her thoughts. "Yes", she began, "I was reared in a God-fearing home and learned to read by reading the Bible, and I have read it front to back. I will not say that I understand it all, but I understand enough to know that God loves me enough to let His Son die in my place. And yes, I prayed for Him to forgive me of my sins and take me to heaven when I die. I just don't particularly wish it to be today."

The reverend Roger Speers chuckled. "Well, child, I can relate to those wishes, as well. I don't feel that my race is run yet either, but in the event that it ends today, I'm okay with that, and I can see that you are, too. All that being said, I feel that I must board that stage. But whatever happens, you must not feel responsible for me, and that's the truth of it. You did the right thing in warning me, and you can rest assured that I will do nothing nor say anything that will jeopardize whatever it is that you and your family are about to attempt."

"What do you mean?" Alaina quizzed. "What makes you think we are going to attempt anything."

"Sweet girl," the reverend explained, "I was here in the cabin with all of you, all night, and I'm not blind, and I'm not deaf, and I'm not dense. And a blind deaf man, by the way, would have been able to feel the electricity in the air in this place. You just watch out for yourself,. and I'll pray that your Lord be with you today."

Alaina suddenly threw her arms around the reverend's waist and hugged him. "Thank you!" she exclaimed as she looked up into his eyes. "Please pray for all of us. We are definitely going to need God's help to pull this off."

"I have to go now," the reverend said as he patted her on the shoulder. "The stage should be arriving any time." With that said, he strolled of in the direction of the train station.

As Alaina entered the cabin, Sheriff Frost was expressing his opinion of how they should continue from here. "We will have to be careful to stay out of sight. If Abernathy or any of that bunch sees us, it will force their hand to react. We don't want that to happen. We are going to be at a great disadvantage. We'll have to wait until they make their move before we can respond. There's no other choice but to stay far enough behind the stage that we can't be seen. If there is any shooting, you ladies need to stay clear. Let Tall and me handle it."

Alaina looked to where her mother sat across the little cabin. As their eyes met, she was sure she caught the slightest smile curling the corners of her mother's lips.

As time neared for the morning train to arrive, the five of them made their way to the stable to ready their horses. Alaina dug the small derringer from her bag and secretly placed it in Rose's hand. Rose, in turn, deposited it into the deep pocket of her coat. Alaina then took the Colt 45 and holster from the bag and began to strap it around her waist.

"Young lady, you heard what I said about staying clear of any shooting didn't you?" Sheriff Frost asked sternly.

"Yes, I heard. I'm just preparing for whatever might happen. My father always told me to prepare for the worst and then you will never be surprised by what happens. Isn't that right, Daddy?"

Tall didn't respond immediately. He only shook his head slightly from side to side knowing he was being set up. Finally, he spoke. "You just pay a mind to what your Uncle Marc says. You have proven that you're quick on your feet when the occasion calls for it. Just promise me you will be careful."

"I promise I'll be careful," she responded, as she looked her father in the eye.

Everyone's attention suddenly turned toward the little depot as a cloud of dust and clatter of horses and harness announced the arrival of the stage. G-String Jack Fulkerson sat on the spring seat of the Concord stagecoach. He methodically swung the coach around with effortless precession alongside the platform of the depot.

"Well, so much for horses hidden in the hills," Sheriff Frost muttered. They all realized what he meant as they counted four deputies riding horseback alongside the stage. "They came mounted already," he continued. "All except the one riding inside with the Pinkertons. Sure would like to know what happened to our young cowboy friends. We could really use their help about now. Guess maybe they decided things were a little too complicated for them."

His eyes moved from Alaina to Rose. "I heard all that conversation between you girls and those two last night. Can't say I blame them for cuttin' out. I can think of a lot of places I'd rather be right now. Just hope they didn't decide it might be more lucrative working for the other outfit."

"I've known those two since they first arrived several years ago," Alaina countered. "I would stake my life on their reputation for honesty and integrity. Whatever they are up to, it is not foul play, I assure you."

No sooner had the Reverend Speers boarded the stage when the first whistle sounded in the distance, signaling the approach of the eastbound train. Staying deep in the shadows inside the stable, the five observers watched the quick and smooth transfer of John Christopher Braunche and his precious baggage from the train onto the stage. Without hesitation, G-String Jack bellowed out with a "Hiyah, gidup there," as he cracked the long, black, snake whip over the heads of the lead team. The stage lurched forward, and in another instant, disappeared back over the same route from which it came.

The road would come to a crossing about a mile from the depot. To the right was Rawlins, to the left Laramie, and straight south was Saratoga and then Encampment. Somewhere within the next forty miles, the phony sheriff and his gang would make their move to steal the bag containing the investment money destined for the smelter plant in Encampment. Where and how were two questions paramount on the minds of five riders who rode slowly away from the stable in cautious pursuit of the southbound stage.

It proved to be a tedious procedure to remain out of sight of the stagecoach and four outriders. The road was straight and flat, for the most part, from the junction to Saratoga. Great care had to be taken to avoid raising a dust cloud that might show their presence. It would not make sense for the outlaws to try anything in this wide-open terrain. The twenty miles between Saratoga and Encampment would be a different situation. There would be cover everywhere.

They could make their move at any point along that stretch of the journey with any number of escape routes. The rougher terrain would lend one advantage for the small group that trailed along, however. It would mean they could close the distance between themselves and the stage without being observed.

The Wolf Hotel in Saratoga was a scheduled stop and gave the little group of pursuers an opportunity to catch up. The busy streets of the little tourist town made it possible to mingle in with the crowd and remain unobserved by the wary Pinkerton agents and the outlaw gang. Saratoga boasted a hot spring and a world renowned, exclusive country club called "Old Baldy." Notoriety from all walks of life came there to relax and escape from their mundane, everyday duties. The resort afforded a boost to the local economy that most small western towns didn't enjoy. Politicians and statesmen, as well as famous performers, could often be seen dining at the Wolf Hotel or strolling along the boardwalks of Saratoga, Wyoming.

After a half hour break to allow the horses to rest and the passengers to refresh themselves, G-String Jack called out for everyone to get back on board. In the brief instant of confused activity, while passengers were boarding and riders were mounting up, the boot on the rear of the stage was lifted ever so slightly, and the coach sank a bit closer to the axel with added weight of a secret cargo that hadn't been there before.

The long black whip snaked out over the lead team once again as the driver yelled his command, and the stage lurched forward, commencing the final leg of its journey. Sheriff Frost and his little posse had stationed themselves a quarter of a mile down the street with a clear view of the Wolf, so they could stay close from here on.

"We probably don't have any worry for the first five miles. They would be foolish to make their move near town," Sheriff Frost offered as they remounted. "Anytime after that would be my guess. The nearer they get to Encampment the more relaxed those two Pinkerton men will become, thinking they have got it made. I'm still thinking right around Cow Creek and that Sleeping Indian rock formation is the most likely place for their heist."

The road became much more accommodating for Sheriff Frost and his riders. Constant hills and curvatures of the road made it possible to follow more closely to the stage. They used great precaution to prevent riding up on them by accident. Tall or the Sheriff would approach each hill crest or curve to assure the stage was not in sight before signaling for the others to proceed. The stage had slowed considerably because of the terrain, making it much easier for them to stay near. The closer they came to Encampment, the more care they took in scouting ahead.

Sheriff Frost had called it perfectly.

When they came to the crest of the hill overlooking Cow Creek, they saw the stage just across the bridge in the little valley below. The passengers, including John Christopher and the two Pinkerton agents, were all standing in a row along the side of the coach. The outlaw deputies were in a circle around the stage with their guns drawn and trained on the passengers.

Another rider had joined them leading a spare horse for the imposter sheriff who had been riding inside the stagecoach until now. He was busy removing the hand cuff that secured the money bag from John Christopher's wrist. Sheriff Frost paused in a moment of indecision as he assessed the situation.

"Okay, Tall and I will ride straight into um, shooting as we go," Marc began. "You girls split up and go to either side under cover of the trees along the creek. Cat you go to one side and let Alaina and Rose go to the other. See if you can give us some gunfire for cover if we get in a tight spot down there, but don't get close enough to get yourselves shot."

Without further hesitation, all five of them crested the hill in a headlong rush for the valley below. Cat slid her saddle gun from its scabbard and veered to the left, Alaina and Rose angled right, and Tall and Sheriff Frost barreled down the hill in a dead run straight for the stage, firing their pistols into the air as they rode.

There are certain circumstances of inevitable, immediate danger that seem to cause time to stand still. This was one of those times. Even while Badger was running headlong through the sagebrush and while she was concentrating on a place to take cover, Alaina was fully aware of what was happening around the stagecoach. The five riders descending the hill and the first volley of shots from Tall and Marc caused an immediate transformation of the entire scene below.

The men on horses who encircled the stage fired a few shots in Marc and Tall's direction and then bunched together around the one with the money bag. At the same time, the cover on the cargo boot on the back of the stage flew open and two men came out with pistols blazing toward the horsemen around the stage, causing three of them to fall to the ground.

The man who had taken the money bag from John Christopher swung into the saddle of his waiting mount and cut a trail west along the far side of the creek with the others hot on his heels. Marc and Tall crossed the bridge and turned in pursuit of the disappearing outlaws who were at least a quarter of a mile in the lead.

Alaina realized Rose had turned to the right along their side of the creek to intercept the fleeing robbers. An instant after she turned to follow her, two men broke through the timber ahead of them and made a break up the steep incline toward the ridge above. Alaina immediately spotted the money bag on the lead horse and recognized the two riders as the two men from Coalville, Utah, the sheriff and the mayor.

A spattering of boulders spilled down the hillside from the rocky ridge above, offering immediate cover for the two men who had split away from the others to try and escape with the money. Rose was riding hard on their heels, determined to not let them get away, with Alaina only a short distance behind. Both girls reined their mounts this way and that around the boulders in hot pursuit, but the steep uphill climb hindered their progress.

They had almost reached the crest when both girls were caught completely off guard by a horse and rider shooting from behind one of the boulders, striking Rose's mare in the shoulder, sending both the mare and Rose tumbling down the incline. Alaina pulled Badger up abruptly while reaching for her pistol but suddenly found herself facing a pair of Winchesters, one trained on her and the other on Rose.

"I should have put a bullet in your head when I had the chance," the outlaw sheriff growled at Rose. "Oh well, now I can finish you both, and good riddance."

The crisp morning air was again shattered by gunfire. Alaina stiffened, expecting the burning pain of hot lead ripping through her body. She realized the sound of the shots came from behind her as she watched the two outlaws topple from their saddles.

Whirling around, she found John Christopher, Tuff, and Sky, all three intently watching to make sure neither of the outlaws posed any further threat. Her eyes focused on the gun in the hands of John Christopher. It looked like nothing she had ever seen before. It was a lever action

Winchester, but both the barrel and the stock had been cut off to leave the rifle not more than eighteen inches long.

Where did that come from? she thought to herself, and then she immediately turned her attention to Rose, who had managed to get to her feet while brushing herself off. A quick inspection of both her and the bay mare revealed only minor scrapes and bruises.

Gunfire in the distance from across the creek brought everyone back to focus. John Christopher retrieved the leather bag containing the money and handed it to Alaina.

"If you will be so kind as to return this to the stage, these two gentlemen and I will assist your father and the sheriff," he said pointing toward Tuff and Sky as he leapt into the saddle.

Without waiting for a response, all three men galloped off in the direction of the gun battle still in progress. The two men on the ground lay motionless. Small blood-soaked spots of dirt underneath each of them indicated their days of "reaping where they had not sown," and their habits of hurting other people to acquire what they wanted were over.

* * *

Alaina and Rose arrived back at the stage and handed the money over to Agent Abernathy who was both relieved and confused by it all.

"I was under the impression that you were part of the plan to take this money," he said to Alaina.

"Yes, well, I'm sorry about that," Alaina began. "Rose and I learned of the scheme to intercept the investment money a few months ago. Then we learned that the men who intended to take it were also the ones who managed to get themselves assigned to ride as security patrol for you. We knew we would not be able to convince you of that, so we had to take measures into our own hands. We didn't count on your arresting Sheriff Frost though."

"Oh, yeah," Abernathy responded, "How do they come to be out of jail, anyway?"

Alaina smiled, "That's a whole other story. We'll fill you in on everything later. Right now, I want to make sure my parents and everyone are all okay." She pointed to the group of riders approaching the stage. The concern that had been evident on her face melted away with great relief as she noted everyone she cared about present and unharmed.

"Did anyone get away?" she quizzed, noting the absence of any of the outlaw gang.

"Not hardly," Sheriff Frost volunteered. "Your English friend here is quite handy with that sawed-off contraption of his."

"Well, I can hardly take the credit," John Christopher chimed in. "These two young Texans are a pair to be reckoned with when there's gunplay. I count myself fortunate to be on their team this time," he finished with a grin.

"Awe, don't be so modest," Tuff responded. "You pretty near hogged all the fun. I think Sky and me are lucky you didn't pull that iron back there in Medicine Bow when we helped Rose and Alaina get you off of that train. I think you were intentionally misleading with your helpless, tenderfoot act."

"Sometimes it works to one's advantage to keep a low profile," John Christopher replied, smiling sheepishly.

"Well, let's continue this jabber-jawing after we get that money to Encampment," Marc broke in. "I'll get some men from the smelter to come clean up this mess," waving toward the corpses around the stage and then to the hills where the others had fallen.

"You all do realize, of course, that there will be consequences to all of the interference with the law," Abernathy remarked. "Taking this money from my possession was illegal, not to mention your breaking out of jail. How did you manage that by the way?"

Everyone pretended not to hear the question as they mounted up to continue toward Encampment. The remainder of the trip proved uneventful. A large crowd had gathered outside the office building at the smelter awaiting the arrival of the stage.

John Christopher retrieved the large leather bag from Agent Abernathy and handed it over to the chairman of the Board of Directors of the Ferris-Haggarty Mine. He was rewarded with an extended applause from the onlookers. After a short speech to convey the appreciation of the owners of the Ferris-Haggerty Mine, the Boston-Wyoming Smelter, and the townspeople of Encampment, the crowd broke up and the rescuers prepared to depart. As John Christopher made his way back to Alaina's side, she turned to him and spoke.

"Paris," she said simply.

"I beg your pardon, Miss… Paris, what?" he responded.

"You said anywhere, any city anywhere, at no expense to me or my family. I choose Paris."

John Christopher laughed. "That I did," he confessed. "Paris it is, then. You arrange the date for your departure with your parents, and I'll secure the proper credentials and tickets for the voyage."

Alaina suddenly realized that he was not jesting. He fully intended to arrange for passage for her and Rose and the entire family to go to Paris for an evening on the town. For the first time in her entire life she found herself to be speechless.

15. THE RECKONING

Alaina and Rose stepped through the door of Dawson's Mercantile in Laramie into the warm Wyoming sunshine. They headed across the boardwalk toward the horse and buggy that was their transportation to take them back to the G Bar G Ranch. Their attention immediately shifted down the street toward the train station and a clattering putt-putting noise that neither of them was familiar with. Curiosity soon turned to amusement as they watched the main street of Laramie suddenly begin transforming from the peaceful serene setting that it normally was to one of chaos and confusion.

Alaina quickly realized that the strange clattering noise was ensuing from one of those new horseless carriages that she had only seen in pictures in newspapers. The confusion, however, arose from the fact that most of the horses in Wyoming rarely read the newspapers and therefore had no appreciation for the modern innovations of mankind, and particularly for a runaway carriage with no horse, making such a god-awful racket. Their reaction was to try, however they could, to get as far away from the clattering contraption as possible.

The trusty animals that had stood quietly along the hitch rails only moments before were now rearing, pawing, nickering, and pulling loose from their moorings to go frantically dashing here and there looking for a route of escape. The ones still transporting their unsuspecting passengers were bolting, bucking, running sideways and backward while riders tried desperately to remain in the saddle or hang on to their reins.

Alaina reached for the tie rope that secured their buggy horse and spoke softly to him while rubbing his nose to keep him calm.

The person managing the automobile seemed to be steering the thing straight toward the spot where Alaina and Rose stood, and as he drew near, he looked vaguely familiar. Most of his entire body was obscured, however. He wore a long linen type duster, a leather hood-style cap on his head, and a pair of goggles covering his eyes. Smudges of dirt dotted the portions of his face that were exposed, but it was the broad toothy smile that demanded Alaina's attention more than anything. As the automobile rolled to a stop a few feet from the two girls, the motorist flipped a switch on the front panel of the machine, shutting the engine off.

"Good morning to you, little sister," came the lighthearted greeting.

"Jesse?" Alaina squealed, "Jesse, is that you?"

"None other," he replied.

Alaina intercepted him as he stepped to the ground and threw her arms around her brother's neck. She clung to him for a long minute before pushing herself away to size him up and down.

"No one told me you were coming home! Why didn't you let me know?"

"No one knew I was coming," Jesse replied. "I have been keeping informed with the proceedings of the court hearings by telephone with Grandma Deborah. I also had a visit from an acquaintance of yours. A Mr. John Christopher Braunche came to the college seeking to retain my services to represent my outlaw family in court. Of course, I declined any stipend, since I am not yet legally qualified to practice law, but I did accept his assistance with travel expenses. So, I am your new legal advisor and assistant. Also, someone named Rose, I take it that might be you," he finished as he directed his gaze toward Rose who had been quietly watching the entire exchange.

"Si, I am Anarosa," she smiled shyly as she extended her hand. "But you should call me Rose if you like. Alaina has done this since we met."

Jesse took her hand in his and lifted it to his lips, giving it a gentle kiss as he smiled in return. "Mr. Braunche forgot to mention your radiant beauty." His eyes sparkled mischievously as he spoke.

"Ahh," Rose responded, "I see that you and Mr. John Christopher Braunche have much in common."

"Oh, how is that?" Jesse came back.

"You each one speak with much flattery," Rose replied laughingly.

"No, no," Jesse corrected. "Flattery is defined as insincere praise. I assure you, Miss Rose, I speak the sincere truth."

"Ahem," Alaina interrupted, "do either of you realize you are not alone?" she teased. "So, what is this thing, anyway?" Alaina quizzed as she motioned toward the automobile.

"That, my dear, is a model 1899 Winton," Jesse began. "This excellent piece of machinery is manufactured in Cleveland, Ohio. It holds the distinction of being top of the line in the industry. It runs on B.F. Goodrich rubber tires and will reach an unprecedented thirty-five miles per hour on a smooth road surface.

"The automobile industry is the wave of the future, my sweet sister. Around the world, people will no longer be limited to public transportation for long distance travel in a reasonable period of time. Eventually there will be a system of roadways connecting cities and towns especially designed for automobiles. It has to happen. It is already happening in the East, and it will ultimately spread across the country. You would do well to invest any available funds you get your hands on in this market, either in autos, in rubber for tires, or in oil and petro. You cannot go wrong by trusting your finances to such a flourishing enterprise. Rest assured that I have."

The commotion on the street had finally subsided, and horse and buggy owners began to gather around the new-fangled apparatus that had interrupted their morning, eying it with suspicion and distrust. Some were not hesitant to voice their disgust. They were not shy about letting it be known, in no uncertain terms, that they would never be caught disrupting God's natural order of things by trading a dependable horse-drawn carriage for such nonsense as a mechanical pile of tin that runs with gears and air inflated rubber.

Jesse only smiled and shook his head with slight disregard, realizing that his birthplace and the people who lived here were at least twenty years behind the more civilized world he was now accustomed to. He was not critical of them, only amused that they somehow thought they would not eventually be swallowed up by the progress of modern industry and lifestyle. Deep down, he longed for the quiet simple pace of life in the West and had determined that the moment he received his degree to practice law from Yale University, he would find the quickest means of transportation back to his home state.

After saying hello to Jules and his Grandma Deborah, Jesse warned everyone that he intended to crank up the auto again, and he, Alaina, and Rose traveled the short distance to the G Bar G across the river from town. He parked the Winton in one of the stalls in the barn where it would remain, for the most part, until he was ready to load it back on a train car for the return trip to Cheyenne.

It was practically useless to him here, as he knew it would be. He had only a few cans of petrol left, and the nearest place to refill them was in Cheyenne. He intended to drive the vehicle from there back to Connecticut after finishing his business here. He had mapped out a route that would allow needed refills for gasoline along the way and was anxious for an adventure across the country at his own leisure. He had been burdened with a strict study schedule for the past three years. The formal studies were finally finished, and he would soon receive a Master of Law Degree. The only thing lacking was the oral examination.

The next few days were both demanding and pleasurable for Jesse. The final court hearing that would decide if the case against his family and Sheriff Frost would go to trial had been set for three days after his arrival in Laramie. The Pinkerton Agency had insisted on pressing charges against Alaina and her family. The charge was interference in matters pertaining to the office of the Federal Marshal. Regardless of the fact that their interference had ultimately reclaimed the stolen money, possibly avoided the murder of Pinkerton agents, John Christopher, and other passengers on the stagecoach.

Jesse had become awfully familiar with how politics seemed to enter into anything that involved the government, whether federal, state, or county. However, he had done his homework before leaving Yale. The library there afforded volumes of books and collections of newspaper articles with reference to the Pinkertons.

The agency had been established by a man named Allan Pinkerton back in 1850. Pinkerton had become famous by supposedly foiling a plot and the first attempt to assassinate Abraham Lincoln. President Lincoln later hired Pinkerton agents for his personal protection during the Civil War. Their popularity grew from there, as did their field of service.

What began as largely investigative work expanded to security guarding and then even to private military exercises. As a result, the number of agents required had mushroomed to the point that they were quickly beginning to rival the numbers of the standing army of the United States itself. This was causing concern with many in state government offices. What could prevent them from being hired as a private army to impose sanctions upon any state in the union? It was a valid concern considering that many of their practices were proven to be shady, if not illegal.

None of that had any bearing upon the matter at hand, of course, but Jesse felt it in the best interest of his family to know every detail about their accuser. He had come to believe that the agency's persistence in pressing this issue was due totally to embarrassment. They simply intended to make an example of Sheriff Frost and Tall and his family to make the public aware that they were well connected in Washington and that any interference with business of theirs would not be tolerated.

Jesse had collected a list of every person that had been involved with the entire escapade, even down to the private passengers on the stage to Encampment. Each one had been contacted, and every one of them agreed to be present for the court hearing in case they were needed as witnesses for the defendants. With those preparations in place, Jesse had felt at ease to spend some time for his own recreation and pleasure.

He, Alaina, and Rose had taken the Winton out for short tours around the country. He had been interested in learning how well it would navigate on the wagon roads and stock trails. Except for an occasional flat tire, which he was prepared for and was able to repair in short order, he was well pleased with its performance. Each of the girls had proven to be apt students in learning to operate the automobile, and they took great pride in realizing that they were probably the first females in the state of Wyoming to have done so.

Rose even insisted that Jesse allow her to drive it down the main street of Laramie, just to watch the reaction of the townsfolk at such an unladylike scene. Neither she nor Jesse figured on the quick response of the editor of the local newspaper. He had set up his camera for a photograph of main street and managed to include the automobile with Rose at the wheel. The photo covered half of the front page of the paper the next day.

And there was Rose, wide-eyed and smiling from ear to ear as she guided the Winton right through the middle of Laramie, Wyoming.

* * *

The morning of the court hearing finally arrived and brought with it, to everyone's surprise, a crowd of spectators. The streets were filled with horses and rigs lined up along the hitch rails on both sides. The seating in the court room quickly filled, and adults and children alike gathered around outside the open windows to witness the proceedings. None of the accused had been required to be locked up, so they all arrived together a quarter of an hour ahead of the time set for the hearing to begin. They took their places in designated seating at the front of the court room to await the judge's arrival.

The bailiff entered the room and immediately announced, "This is a grand jury hearing of the first district court of the State of Wyoming with the Honorable David Thiel presiding. All rise." Everyone stood as the judge entered and took his position on the bench.

"This hearing is now in session," Judge Thiel began. "Let everyone be reminded that this is not a trial but rather a hearing to determine if there are grounds for a trial. There are several issues to be considered. We will examine them one at a time. Mr. Abernathy is here to represent the Pinkerton Agency and requests no legal counsel to assist him. Mr. Johnson, I understand, is a graduating student at Yale School of Law and will represent the suspects.

"Mr. Abernathy, you will be allowed to state each of your employer's claims in turn, and then Mr. Johnson, for the suspects, will be allowed to respond.

"The first issue before this court is the claim that a large amount of investment money was illegally taken from your possession, Mr. Abernathy, and involves the two young women, Alaina and Rose, as well as two young cowboys referred to in your report as Tuff and Sky. Is that correct?"

"Yes, your Honor," Abernathy responded. "Two other Pinkerton agents and myself were escorting a courier, Mr. John Christopher Braunche, and a large sum of money to be delivered to the smelter plant in Encampment, Wyoming, when we were bushwhacked in the streets of Medicine Bow by gunmen that were hired by them," he stated, pointing to Alaina and

Rose. "The courier, as well as the money, was taken from our possession at that time."

"Mr. Johnson, do you wish to respond to these allegations?" Judge Thiel inquired.

"Yes, your Honor. If it please the court, I would recognize Mr. John Christopher Braunche, the courier referred to by Mr. Abernathy, and explain to the court that the investment money in question was never out of the possession of its rightful owner. In fact, Your Honor, the money belonged, in its entirety, to Mr. Braunche and was never out of his possession except for a brief period when he requested that these two young ladies, Miss Alaina and Miss Rose, return it to Mr. Abernathy. Mr. Braunche, at the time, was assisting in the apprehension of the outlaws who were the real culprits in this whole thing.

"The stagecoach that was transporting Mr. Braunche and the money had just been held up by a group of outlaws imposing as lawmen. Outlaws, I might add, that had been hired by Mr. Abernathy to escort the stage and the money to its destination. We contend, therefore, that no crime was committed by these two young ladies, and Mr. Braunche has agreed to testify to that fact, if the need arises."

"Since this is a grand jury," Judge Thiel began, "I'll not call non-party witnesses to the stand. For my own peace of mind in determining the truth here, I would ask Mr. Braunche to stand." John Christopher immediately obliged. "Mr. Braunche, a simple yes or no will suffice. Do you agree that the statement just presented by Mr. Johnson, counsel for the defendants, is true in its entirety?"

"Yes, Your Honor. Everything he said is the truth," John Christopher responded.

An expression of total shock suddenly replaced the cocky confidence that had been evident on Abernathy's face until now. The shock soon gave way to anger, and then to determination—determination to put the young law student in his place.

"Very well." Judge Thiel continued, "That being the case, I see no need for further investigation of that point.

"The next allegation against the suspects has to do with the alleged jail break and involves all of them, Sheriff Frost, Deputy Tall Johnson, Cat

Johnson, Alaina Johnson, Anarosa Torres, and these two young men you call Sky and Tuff.

"Mr. Abernathy, it is your claim that, as a deputy of the office of the United States Marshal, you acted upon the request of said office and placed District Sheriff Marc Frost and his deputy, Mr. Tall Johnson, under arrest for interfering with matters pertaining to the office of the United States Marshal. You then claim that the two men before mentioned were illegally removed from their cell by the two young gentlemen, Tuff and Sky, who pretended to have been sent to escort them to be held here in Laramie at the federal penitentiary. Is that correct?"

"That is correct," Abernathy began, "but that is not all, Your Honor. The two young men posing as a sheriff and deputy from here in Laramie, used a forged telegram, supposedly from the U.S. Marshal's office in Washington, to convince another agent, who was under my supervision at the time, to release Sheriff Frost and Mr. Tall Johnson into their custody."

"Is the other agent that you are referring to in this court room?" Judge Thiel inquired.

"No, your honor," Abernathy replied. "He is on assignment in another state at this time."

"Do you have the telegram that you allege to have been forged?" the judge questioned.

"Again…no, Your Honor," he confessed as he lowered his head. "We suspect that those two men, Sky and Tuff, took it with them when they left the jail that day."

"Mr. Johnson, do you wish to speak to these allegations concerning unlawful release of the prisoners Sheriff Frost and Mr. Tall Johnson?" Judge Thiel asked.

"Yes, Your Honor," Jesse responded. "Sheriff Frost, as you know, is a district sheriff duly appointed by the state of Wyoming. My father, Tall Johnson, was a sworn deputy at the time Agent Abernathy placed them under arrest. Also, at that time, Agent Abernathy informed Sheriff Frost that he was acting on orders from the U.S. Marshal's office in Washington D.C.

"Your Honor, I paid a visit to the U.S. Marshal's office in Washington while in route to Laramie from Connecticut. No one in that office had any knowledge of a directive to place a Wyoming district sheriff under arrest.

In fact, they informed me that they have no authority to do such a thing. I have in my possession a signed affidavit to that effect. We contend that the arrest of Sheriff Frost and his deputy was unlawful and unwarranted, and therefore, there was no crime committed in their release."

"May I have a look at that affidavit, Mr. Johnson?" the judge requested.

Jesse approached the bench and handed the paper up for him to inspect. After looking it over carefully, he handed it back.

"I am satisfied with the authenticity of the document in Mr. Johnson's possession. Mr. Abernathy, do you have anything you wish to say in response to Mr. Johnson's claims?" Judge Thiel asked.

"No, Your Honor." Abernathy stated flatly.

"In that case, I believe I have heard enough," Judge Thiel began. "In light of the fact that, were it not for the two young ladies sitting before me, Mr. Abernathy, you could be dead at this very moment, and not only you but Mr. Braunche, and possibly other innocent bystanders. At the very least, the large sum of money that was placed in your charge would have been lost.

"These good citizens of Wyoming, upon whom you have brought these outrageous charges, have done nothing but assist you, and so far as I can ascertain, have done nothing illegal. In other words, Mr. Abernathy, you, and your agency have succeeded only in wasting the time of this court and these good people.

"Consider yourself fortunate that this is not a trial, for if it were, I would see you and your employer responsible for, not only the court costs, but reimbursement for all expenses for counsel, for the defendants, as well as for Mr. Braunche. You might also find yourself on trial for filing false charges. Mr. Abernathy, if you ever appear in my court room again it had better be for legitimate reasons. Is that quite clear, Sir?"

"Yes, Your Honor." Agent Abernathy conceded.

"As for you, young man," the judge continued, turning his gaze directly upon Jesse, "Your manner and precision in handling this matter is very impressive. You obviously have a great future ahead of you. I am fully aware that your mother could have represented herself and the rest of the accused in this hearing, and I commend her for placing her confidence in you. As far the allegations against these suspects, I find no evidence that would call for an indictment. Therefore, this hearing is dismissed, and the accused are cleared of all charges and are free to go."

16. Settling Old Scores

Alaina and Rose rode along side by side on the rough mountainous trail that crossed from Vernal, Utah, to Frank and Martha Dodd's ranch. Everything looked entirely different from the last time they had passed this way. The icy world of a mountain winter had given way to lush green grass in the high parks and meadows.

An occasional encounter with a deer or elk told them that the wildlife had moved back to higher elevations to enjoy the cool mountain climate and the vegetation that was now available there. Looking up at the position of the sun, Alaina reckoned that it was about mid-day and began searching for a likely place to stop for lunch. Locating a small spring-fed stream, she pulled Badger to a stop and loosened the saddle girth as she waited for her mom and dad to catch up. Rose followed her lead and then helped Alaina prepare a makeshift picnic table atop a large flat rock.

"How much farther to the Dodd place?" Tall asked, as he brought the carriage to a halt. He and Cat were seated in a bright new Studebaker carriage he had purchased, along with the harness, just before leaving Laramie. The Studebaker Company had offered a cut-rate price since they were liquidating inventory of horse-drawn vehicles to gear up for production of Studebaker automobiles.

A gentle smile curled the corners of Tall's mouth as a mischievous thought crept into his mind. Judging by the wagon trail they were traveling, Tall guessed it would be some time before the Dodd's would have roads to accommodate a horseless carriage. Perhaps the executives of Studebaker should travel their homeland more extensively. They might find it in their best interests to reconsider their marketing techniques.

"I guess two to three hours," Alaina answered. "It's hard to tell. We were not following the wagon trail when we came across, but we had to skirt the deep snow drifts. It was an all-day trip under those conditions, but I think we are making good progress today. Frank and Martha will be really surprised that you two came with us."

"Well, I feel like it is the least we can do, considering how kind they treated the two of you, being complete strangers and all," Tall returned. "I hope he will accept this rig and team without too much fuss. It's a small token of our appreciation as far as I'm concerned, but some folks are shy about any gesture that might seem like charity."

Cat brought a basket from the carriage and began laying out bread and meat they had purchased in Vernal. "I really don't think he will have a choice unless he wants to drive it all the way back to Laramie," she added.

The two horses, Sassy and Trooper, tied to the back of the carriage would be Tall and Cat's transportation back home. Tall had handpicked two large bay mares to provide a good matched team for Frank Dodd. They were especially suited for all-around farm and ranch work. Not only could they be used in harness, but as saddle horses and as broodmares. They would each produce a fine foal early next spring, sired by Alaina's stallion, Badger. Frank and Martha Dodd would have a classy means of transportation, a strong team of work horses, and a start for a fine horse breeding operation.

After a leisurely meal and welcomed rest from their long journey, the four travelers continued making their way over the pass to the west. It was about mid-afternoon when they came to the last mountain ridge above the Dodd place.

As they broke over the top to begin their decent into the valley, Tall suddenly pulled the team to a stop. An expression of utter unbelief swept across his face as he looked at the scene before him. Visions from years long past rushed into his mind. There were no teepees now, and there were cattle instead of Indian ponies scattered along both sides of the river, but other than that, the valley seemed unchanged in every other way.

Almost thirty years had passed since the small Indian party had stopped in almost this very place, and he had looked down into this valley for the first time. A sudden melancholy came over him as he pictured himself astride a spotted Indian pony with the strong arms of Chief Red Falcon encircling him, gazing down at a busy Indian village below.

"Tall, are you okay?" Cat had broken the silence as she noticed the expression on his face.

"I don't know." Those were the only words he could seem to utter at the moment. He sat transfixed while a rush of memories paraded through his head. How many times had he ridden off of this ridge into the valley below? Once, he remembered, near the end, there was a battle playing out, as he and his party of young braves returned from gathering wild horses.

"Tall," Cat spoke with urgency in her voice, realizing now that something was definitely amiss. "What is going on?"

"This is it," Tall heard himself utter. "This is where the Indian village was."

Cat, Alaina and Rose listened intently as Tall described what it had been like the first time he had entered this valley and then how circumstances had changed for him as time passed. This had been his home during those formative years of late adolescence and early manhood. He realized that much of the grit that he had within him was a result of his experiences here in this valley.

The parade of emotions that he was feeling did not include anger or self pity. He was, however, thankful for the good fortune of having been rescued from his captors by what he considered to be an act of God.

This unexpected discovery of his former home was somewhat mind-boggling, but Tall quickly recovered his composure, and the four of them dropped off of the ridge and continued along the road toward the log cabin in the distance. But long before they arrived, they realized they were being observed by two lonely figures.

Frank and Martha Dodd seldom had visitors to their little hidden valley, and never had they seen a group of travelers arriving together like those coming now. They stood with their hands shading their eyes, trying to determine if they could recognize anyone in the party. Rose and Alaina nudged their mounts into a long canter and entered the little barnyard well ahead of Tall and Cat.

Frank and Martha's surprise was evident as they all greeted one another with smiles and hugs. Alaina had plenty of time to inform the young couple about who was in the carriage, so her mom and dad received a warm welcome upon their arrival, as well. After introductions and a brief visit, the animals were cared for and put away for the day. The subject of the team and carriage was brought up out of curiosity from the Dodd's.

"I know it ain't polite to ask questions of folks ye jist become acquainted with," Frank began, "But I jist been wonderin' about these extree horses. Don't appear to me that ye all been ridin' all that hard to git here, that ye'ed need to switch off."

Tall chuckled softly. "Well, Mr. Dodd…"

"Ye can jist call me Frank. Makes me a bit uncomfortable to be addressed as mister by someone who is my elder and plainly a lot wiser than myself," Frank insisted.

"Okay, Frank." Tall continued, "I have been hesitant to mention the horses because I wasn't quite sure how to approach the subject. You see, we, myself, my wife, and Alaina and Rose wanted to show our appreciation to you and Martha for being so kind and helpful to our girls when they came through here back in the winter. You really don't know the full story yet, but you will, and your assistance could well have decided their success or failure in making it back home safely. The carriage and team of mares are for you and Martha, a token of our gratitude."

"And that is not all," Cat broke in hurriedly, "Martha, I have some special things just for you. Alaina and Rose described the solitude of your ranch and how infrequently you are able to go into the settlement. I hope you don't mind that I brought some grocery provisions from the mercantile in Vernal."

Cat lowered her voice as she continued. "I apologize for my failure to realize your condition." Her gaze softly fixed on Martha's midsection and the obvious development of the new life there. "I guessed at your dress size from what the girls told me, but I'm afraid you will have to put it away and save it for a later date."

Tears began to well up in Martha's eyes as she rushed to give Cat another hug and thank her for her kind thoughtfulness.

"What we had in mind," Tall went on, "is to stay a few days and help with your spring roundup, if we aren't too late."

"No, by jingles, yer jist in time, and I didn't have any idy how I was gonna manage it, Martha bein' in a family way and all," Frank blurted with a widening grin.

The afternoon passed quickly with incredible stories being told about Alaina and Rose's adventures and Tall's early years being spent right in this very valley. They strolled down along the river with Tall, pointing out the location of the teepees and explaining what life was like with the Indians. Then making their way back to the cabin, sleeping arrangements were discussed, and then the ladies began preparations for the evening meal while Tall and Frank went to the barn to see to the evening chores. When they were out of earshot of the house, Frank began to explain to Tall the dilemma he found himself in.

"I'm in way over my head, Tall," he began. "I thought I could make a go of it out here, but I'm 'bout ready to give it up. It's too much for one man, and I can't afford to hire help. Rustlers from over around Brown's Hole keep running my stock off, an' I can't watch over 'em all day and night.

"Instead o' roundin' up for brandin', I jist about as soon we round up and ye all help me drive what's left of the herd to market. Martha and me have been talkin' 'bout jist loadin' up what we can in the wagin and goin' back down to Arkansas where our folks is."

Tall stopped in his tracks. This bit of news had taken him entirely by surprise. Frank turned toward him, and as their eyes met, Tall could tell he was dead serious.

"Let me give it some thought," Tall finally replied. "There has to be a better solution than for you and your family to lose your entire investment here."

They fed all of the animals, and Tall gathered eggs from the nests in the barn while Frank coaxed the milking cow out of a pail of fresh milk. They were ready to return to the cabin when Tall spoke up.

"Frank, if you and Martha are dead set on going back south, I can't fault you for it. I am prepared to make you an offer, and you could stay here or you could go…either way.

"I'll pay you a fair price for your livestock and for your spread. You could stay and manage the place, and I could send help to you. Or if you decide to go, I know some young men that I believe would come and look after things for me here. Either way, and even if you decide you want to hang on to the place, I think I have a connection that would solve the rustling problem.

"Why don't you discuss it with Martha tonight, and tomorrow we will begin gathering the cattle. By the time we get them brought in, you can let me know what you have decided. If you decide you want to hang on, we will put your brand on them. If you decide you want to sell, we will burn my brand on them. How does that sound?"

"That sounds like a real good plan, Tall." Frank said, grinning from ear to ear.

The evening was spent around the table, first enjoying a fine meal topped off with strong black coffee brewed from fresh ground beans brought from Vernal. While the ladies cleared the table and tidied up, more stories were shared. The two families grew in kinship with one another, the kind of kinship and closeness that the wide expanses of the mountains tend to spawn out of the sheer need for human companionship and camaraderie. Finally, Tall reached for the gold watch he carried in his vest pocket and reluctantly spoke up.

"I hate to break up such a festive occasion, but if we are going to accomplish any work tomorrow, we'll be needing to get some rest."

The next several days were almost like replays of each other. The entire valley was combed for every last cow, calf, and maverick. Each evening concluded with everyone bringing their catch for the day back to the herd that was formed between the river and the barn.

After the first herd was brought in, Cat volunteered to hold them together while Tall, Frank, and the two girls teamed up in pairs to scour the surrounding hills and valleys for strays. Martha prepared meals and tidied up afterwards.

By the time everything was ready for the branding, Frank and Tall had clued everyone in on the decision that the Dodd's were about to make. It was carried right down to the kindling of the branding fires before the answer was given.

Frank had quizzed Tall about what kind of plans he might have for his ranch if he were to sell it to him. He even asked what brand he would use. Tall answered his questions as best he could without much thought as to why Frank was so curious. But while Tall and Cat were busy with final preparations in the corral, he slipped away and found Martha, and the two of them came back together bearing an iron with a Teepee shaped brand on it like Tall had described to him.

It consisted of two slanted lines crossing near the top. One then had a line across the top of it to form a "T," and the other, had a line that circled around to form a "P." The result was the shape of a Teepee formed with the letters "T" and "P."

"Martha wants to raise our children back home with our kin," Frank began, "so we want to give you this here iron to seal our decision. We will sign the deed for the homestead over to you, and you can decide on a fair price. We were figgerin' to jist leave it, so we will be more than satisfied with whatever your price.

"As for the cattle, I wouldn't a been able to gather half this many without help. The rest would have been claimed by neighboring ranches or thieves. I figure the whole herd might average twelve dollars a head at the market. I'll be more 'n happy with ten dollars a head for them that's got my brand and calves that pair up with um. The mavericks are yours for all of the work you and your family have done to help us out. Ifin that's agreeable with you."

"Well, I'll check at the land office and determine the value of your homestead. I'll agree to your proposition on the condition that you take the carriage and two mares back to Arkansas, along with a young stallion that I will select and ship to you after you settle down there. I will also pay for train shipment of whatever you wish to take with you. Is that agreeable?"

Tall held out his hand to seal the deal and the two men shook on it.

"Okay, now that's settled, let's get to it!" Alaina shouted. "I need to get back to Laramie."

Tall and Cat gave each other a knowing glance.

Rose giggled and then made her contribution. "Si, Mister John Christopher will be wondering where you are and why you have not telephoned," she said teasingly.

Alaina felt her face flush at the teasing remark but had no reply, for Rose's observation was too near correct. John Christopher had telephoned at least once every week since he had returned to Europe.

Three days later the branding was completed. Frank and Martha's personal items were loaded onto a boxcar in Green River, including the carriage and team of mares. Tall had arranged for Sky and Tuff to come to Utah to manage the new ranch there. Tall had decided he would call it The Indian Valley Ranch, but when he transferred ownership he secretly deeded it to Alaina Marie Johnson.

Since the Dodd's would travel east to Cheyenne and then south to Denver, they all boarded the train together in Green River and enjoyed a leisurely day of comfort in the Pullman coach. Alaina and Rose laughed as they told the Dodd's about their last train excursion from Green River to Rawlins in not so comfortable accommodations.

Upon arrival in Laramie, the Johnsons bid goodbye to the Dodd's after making them promise to telephone or write as soon as the baby arrived. Alaina waited for the train to pull away and waved one last time to her special friends and then hurried toward Dawson's Mercantile. After a quick hug for her Grandma Deb, she ran to the phone and began to turn the crank to reach the operator.

"He's not in his office," her Grandma offered. "There are instructions on the note pad as to how to reach him, but he won't be arriving there until tomorrow. Nice to see you, too, by the way," her Grandma chided smilingly.

Alaina placed the receiver back in its cradle and turned to the notepad. The message filled the entire page and included a number where he could be reached in Paris. He would be there for a few months on business and had arranged for steamboat passage for Alaina and her family, including Rose and Jesse, to meet him there at their earliest convenience.

* * *

The ocean liner, *Campania*, was every young lady's dream of a perfect cruise ship. The captain had somehow picked Alaina and Rose out of the hundreds of passengers on board and made it his mission to show them every inch of the magnificent craft, as well as explain all the mechanics. Jesse refused to be left behind. Alaina suspected that was for reasons other than his interest in mechanics, but his unending questions kept the captain going for hours explaining the triple expansion engines and twin-screw propellers and how the *Campania* held the "Blue Riband" award for making the fastest North Atlantic crossing on record.

Alaina and Rose were much more impressed with the luxurious décor and fantastic accommodations. The first-class public rooms and suite staterooms were paneled with oak and mahogany with thickly carpeted floors and richly upholstered furniture with velvet curtains hanging beside the windows and portholes. Alaina's favorite, however, was the magnificent dining saloon. She estimated it to be at least seventy feet wide and a hundred feet long, and over the central part was a well that rose up through three decks to a skylight above.

Each evening their dining experience was enhanced by lovely classical music from a stringed band. Alaina and Rose practically wore Jesse to a frazzle by insisting that he dance with them in turn. Alaina could tell that Rose was having the time of her life. The only thing that could have made it more rewarding for herself would have been the presence of John Christopher, and the only reason she waited excitedly for the cruise to come to an end was her vision of his smiling face waiting for her in Paris.

It was early morning of the sixth day when the *Campania* began its maneuver through the estuary of the Seine River. The final leg of the journey would be slower but much more scenic, for they would continue up the Seine to the Port of Rouen where they would meet John Christopher. Then the following day they would travel by train to Paris, "La Ville-Lumière" ("The City of Light").

Alaina trembled with excitement as they neared the Port of Rouen. As far back as she could remember, from the first time she had read about France and Paris, she had dreamed of one day visiting there. And now, because of John Christopher, her dream was coming true. To top it off, John Christopher was waiting for her there.

She suddenly felt her cheeks warm with a blush of embarrassment. Until a few months ago, a man was the farthest thing from her mind. Dozens of young men had vied for her attention, but each one found themselves hopelessly rejected. It was not because she thought none were good enough for her. There was just never that spark she had heard her mother describe when speaking of how she felt about her father. John Christopher, however, was an entirely different matter. From their first eye contact on the train from Laramie to Medicine Bow all those months ago, she had been smitten, and she knew it.

At first, she had not known what to make of it, but as the days and weeks passed, she realized the feelings she had were turning into something very special. And now she was convinced that she would go to the ends of the earth to be with him and wanted them never to be apart.

The other conflicting feeling she was having, though, was the possibility that John Christopher didn't feel the same about her. Her suspicion was that he did, but he had never said as much. Even though they talked frequently by phone, and he had gone to great expense to bring her and her family to Paris, the possibility gnawed at her that all of that was just to honor the promise he had made to her back at the line shack. She knew that, above all, John Christopher was a man of his word. He would honor any promise he made to anyone.

That thought caused the trembling to escalate a degree or two, for the possibility of not having John Christopher in her life was something she was not ready to consider.

Mounting activity on the main deck and the deafening blare of the ships horn suddenly jolted Alaina back to reality. They were entering the Port of Rouen. When the announcement was made for passengers to prepare to disembark, Alaina hurried to their cabin to gather up her luggage.

She smiled as she thought back to the days she and Rose spent in the cave and her resolution to never leave on a journey without her lariat. She chuckled to herself as she conceded to the fact that she had not brought her lariat, but it seemed that she had brought everything else she owned.

With assistance of a luggage cart and a bellboy, she and Rose finally joined the others at the boarding ramp just as the ship was being moored to the dock. Alaina's gaze swept the crowd looking for a familiar face. There he was in full view. He had already picked her out in the crowd and was waving frantically to gain her attention. She waved back, jumping up and down with excitement as she pushed through the crowd to the front of the line, oblivious to any protest that might have been voiced. Nothing mattered except that man on the dock who seemed just as excited to see her as she was to see him.

The ramp slid into place, the attendant removed the barrier, and Alaina found herself in John Christopher's arms. They clung to one another for a long moment, and then after a searching gaze into one another's eyes, their lips met in a tender kiss that was more of a surprise to the two of them than to anyone else.

After a clumsy attempt to discount what had just happened, John Christopher began greeting the others. Cat and Rose gave him a welcoming hug and Tall and Jesse a warm handshake, after which he directed them to a motor car parked nearby that would transport them to their hotel.

* * *

The next two weeks were like a perfect dream of a European excursion. John Christopher proved to be a superb tour guide for both fabulous cities of Rouen and Paris. In Rouen, they visited the Notre Dame cathedral, with its *Tour de Beurre* (Butter Tower), and Claude Monet's paintings, as well as botanical gardens dating back sixty years, and the place where Joan of Arc was burned at the stake.

All were places Alaina had read about in travel brochures and magazines and determined to one day visit if ever given the opportunity. However, all of that paled in relation to Paris. Her mind was spinning with excitement as she experienced places and sites she had only dreamed of seeing one day.

Their tour began with the Eiffel Tower and then on to the Louvre, one of the largest museums in the world with famous sculptures and paintings, including the Mona Lisa. They walked through the Tuileries Gardens and the Champs-Elysees, which is known as "the most beautiful avenue in the world," and led them to the Arc de Triomphe that is centered in what resembles the spokes of a wheel—twelve avenues reaching out to all parts of the city.

Their days included times when they were all together, but there were also shopping sprees for the ladies, at which times the men conveniently found other ways to occupy themselves. They often paired off to explore in different directions, meeting up for meals at various cafés and diners.

There was so much to see and enjoy, Alaina thought she might "gaze her eyes out," as her grandmother used to say, before the two weeks were up. John Christopher surprised them all one evening after dinner with the announcement that they would travel to Normandy for the final few days of their time together.

The following morning, they boarded a train headed northwest from Paris. Their passage was for the city of Dieppe, located on the plateau Pays de Caux, (Pei de Ko). On arrival, John Christopher made a phone call from the train station, and shortly thereafter, a large motor car arrived to take them to their destination.

"Welcome to Chateau de la Braunche," John Christopher offered, as he stepped from the automobile. "It has been in my family for centuries," he explained.

The castle sat perched near the edge of a steep white cliff that dropped straight down into the crashing waves of the English Channel and looked exactly like Alaina would have pictured a fairy tale castle. The hills surrounding were covered by the huge vineyard that had supported the estate for the past hundred years. There were wineries and storage buildings filled with rows and rows of barrels of aging wine, along with small housing structures for the workers and tool sheds for the harvesting carts and gathering baskets. The entire scene looked peaceful and serene…like a picture on the cover of a travel magazine.

"Dover is directly across the Channel," John Christopher continued, "And the cliffs there are identical to these, thus the name "White Cliffs of Dover." It is my greatest pleasure to have all of you reside here for the remainder of your stay, however long that may be. The journey from here to London is only a matter of hours, as it is from here to Paris, which makes it very convenient for me working in both cities.

If you will extend your stay a week longer, I will escort you to London and show you the sights there, as well. However, tomorrow is a special day for a special someone if I am not mistaken. Am I correct in my recollection that tomorrow is your eighteenth birthday, Miss Alaina?"

Alaina blushed, "How did you remember that? It's been months since I told you."

"It is one of the more important dates on the annual calendar," John Christopher said smiling. "I have prepared a surprise for you. I have arranged for a party with a dinner and an orchestra for dancing afterward. However, my special surprise is for you to meet my family. They will arrive on the ferry tomorrow morning."

Alaina stood speechless. Her mom and dad, Jesse, and Rose all began to clap and wish her a happy birthday. John Christopher pulled her close and held her as tears welled in her eyes and trickled down her cheeks.

"I don't know what to say," she finally uttered. "This has to be the best birthday of my entire life. Well, maybe except for the first one."

They all laughed.

The following day was one of mixed feelings for Alaina. She was excited beyond words that John Christopher had been so thoughtful as to plan a birthday party for her and that he wanted her to meet his family. On the other hand, she was a bundle of nerves.

Questions continued to present themselves in a very disconcerting fashion. What if they did not like her? What if she made a fool of herself in their presence and embarrassed her family as well as John Christopher? There were those "what-if's" again. They seemed to always be there in the recesses of her mind and then boldly presenting themselves to confuse her at the most inopportune moment.

Rose could tell she was troubled and tried to calm her. "You don't be worried, *mi amiga*," she comforted. "You weel be fine. Who would not see you as everyone sees you? You are *piedra preciosa*. You are *una joya*, a jewel. They weel see it. You don't be worried."

Alaina smiled as she hugged her. Rose was like a sister to her. They had hardly been apart since the day Alaina had discovered her lying beside that stream. It seemed like ages ago now. Rose had completely recovered physically and almost completely emotionally from the ordeal. She still had moments, of course, when she thought about her brother and the tragedy of his needless death. But underneath the sadness was the satisfaction of knowing that his death had been avenged, and the one who took her brother's life had been brought to justice.

Dressed in her long flowing evening gown, she was beautiful. She reminded Alaina of the paintings she had seen of Spanish princesses. She looked elegant. She was also intelligent. She had enrolled in the girl's school in Laramie and had finished one course of study before they left for New York to come on this trip. She planned to continue with education and become a schoolteacher. Alaina had no doubt that she would succeed.

John Christopher's family had arrived. Alaina had watched from the window in the tower off of her and Rose's bedroom. She saw a tall stately gentleman and two very regal looking ladies dismount the auto and enter the chateau. That was when her nerves attacked unmercifully, leaving a nauseating feeling in the pit of her stomach.

She had been in the middle of preparing herself for the evening and had not dared go down to meet them in her state of mind. She was not at all certain that she wouldn't be sick. A sudden knock on the door startled her back to the present. Rose opened the door for Cat to come in.

"You look lovely, dear," she said immediately. "Everyone has arrived, and it's time for you to come out of hiding," she smiled, knowing what was going on in her daughter's head.

She remembered perfectly that day so many years ago when a young man came to the college in Saint Louis to take her out on the town. The evening ended with a proposal and the beginning of true happiness for her, but the turmoil within her beforehand tied her gut in knots. *What we girls go through for our men!* she thought to herself as she patted Alaina on the shoulder.

"You'll be fine," she continued, "Rose and I are right here with you."

The long winding stairway led into a large foyer that was connected to a huge parlor on one side and a dining hall almost as large on the other. The dining table stretched throughout the hall and was decorated in exquisite style with garnishing and candles amid pieces of fine china and large dishes of food, many of which the American visitors had never seen. All looked deliciously appealing.

A large crowd of guests surrounded the table waiting for her arrival. John Christopher strolled across the foyer and took her hand as she reached the landing. Placing her arm in his, he escorted her into the dining hall and directly to his family.

"Mr. and Mrs. Johnson, Jesse and Rose, would you kindly join us?" he invited. After they all gathered around, he continued. "Mother, Father, Emiline, allow me to present a dear family from the western frontier of the United States of America. Were it not for these brave souls, I very well may not be alive for this joyous occasion.

"This is Tall and Emma Cathrine Johnson and their son, Jesse Johnson. The young lady beside Jesse is Anarosa Torres whose life was miraculously saved by this one I hold on my arm, and whom I also hold in my heart. This is Alaina Marie Johnson, the special guest for the evening and the reason for the occasion, I might add, for today is her eighteenth birthday."

Everyone clapped and the guests all smiled and nodded to her.

"Alaina, Rose, Cat, Jesse and Tall, I present my father, Sir Richard Braunche, my mother, Christina Braunche, and my sister, Emiline Braunche."

The men all shook hands in turn and expressed their pleasure in the meeting. The ladies were greeted with a tender kiss on the back of the hand, as was the proper and genteel custom in Normandy.

After the formalities, John Christopher continued, "In the interest of time, I will not attempt to name each of the other guests but will gladly introduce you after we have dined. So, with the formalities behind us, let us be seated, and as you are so fond of saying in your country, 'let's dig in.'"

Everyone laughed as they took their places around the table.

The evening proved to be a gala event. Dinner was indescribable and was topped off with scrumptious deserts served in individual dishes to each guest in turn. Then a waiter entered the room with a giant birthday cake sporting eighteen lighted candles. He placed it on the table before Alaina while the orchestra played and the guests honored her by singing "for she's a jolly good fellow". John Christopher then rose from his chair and requested the first dance of the evening.

The orchestra stuck up a lively waltz as he escorted Alaina into the large parlor, and they entertained the crowd in perfect ballroom style. After a time of dancing and visiting with the Braunches and other guests, John Christopher took Alaina by the hand and led her out through a garden filled with roses and beautiful beds of multicolored flowers and up a long stairway to a large balcony situated between two towers.

The night was perfect. The sky sparkled with a million stars. A warm south breeze carried the faint salty fragrance of the English Channel. The soft rhythm of the waves lapping against the cliffs emanated soothingly around them as they stood together gazing at a full moon reflecting off the water.

John Christopher slowly dropped to one knee as he moved his hand into a jacket pocket and brought out a bright shinny object between his finger and thumb.

"Alaina Marie Johnson," he began hesitantly, "would you make me the happiest man in the entire world by agreeing to be my lifelong companion? Will you marry me?"

Alaina had not even dared to dream of such a thing happening on this night. Being caught completely off guard brought with it a slight hesitation as she tried to reassure herself that she had heard him correctly. John Christopher took it as indecision on her part and quickly continued.

"I realize this is sudden, and perhaps I should have prepared you more adequately. I did take the liberty to approach your father concerning my feelings for you and assuring him of my honorable intentions. He gave me his blessing, indicating that he would be pleased to have me as part of his family…"

His voice trailed off as Alaina took his hand and lifted him to his feet. She then placed her finger over his lips gently shushing him. "Yes," she responded, "Yes, I will marry you. I wasn't expecting this. I dared not even dream of it. But you have just made my life complete. I love you, John Christopher Braunche."

"And I love you, Alaina Marie Johnson, soon to be Braunche." They laughed together, and then John Christopher pulled her close and held her in a long tender embrace.

After allowing themselves half an hour to enjoy and to adjust to what had just happened, the newly engaged couple made their way back inside. When the orchestra broke to get refreshments, John Christopher called for everyone's attention.

"Friends, guests and family, if you would allow me, I would like to make an announcement." He reached for Alaina and drew her to his side. "This young lady has just made this the happiest day of my life by agreeing to be my wife."

The room broke out in applause and shouts of approval, followed by a rush to personally congratulate them.

"I believe this justifies a step up in the libations," Sir Richard called from across the room. "Where is that reserve run you so greedily hold on to? Send for the good stuff, son, and let's have a toast…a toast to your good fortune after all these years."

"Father, if you would indulge me", John Christopher began. "Friends and family, I must have you realize that customs and convictions are quite different in the part of the world from which the Johnsons hail. For some, even the slightest imbibing is considered to be unchristian. Let us not frown upon their dedication to their moral principles. I, for one, do not wish to be the cause for any God-fearing person to stumble. So, waiters and waitresses, if you would be so kind as to refill the water goblets so that all of our guests can, in good conscience, raise their glass to a toast. After all, it's not what is in the glass but rather what is in the heart that insures that a toast is meaningful and memorable."

John Christopher reached for a goblet and all glasses were lifted in sync as his voice rang out above the rest, "Here is to my new family, to happiness, to fulfilled dreams, and to the best of times."

The room exploded with cheers and applause.

Epilogue

Tall reached for the handbrake as the motorcar rolled to a gentle stop. Several minutes passed as his eyes swallowed in the entire panorama of rugged mountainous terrain that sprawled before him. Cat sat across from him in the passenger's seat almost as spellbound as he.

So much had changed in the few short years since they traveled this path together before, but so much more since Tall had perused this valley for the first time. He vividly recalled, as he had at least a million times before, a wide-eyed, frightened ten-year-old boy who had suddenly been ripped from his world and thrown into another, clutching tightly to a red-skinned man he didn't know, and who, he was almost certain, meant to do him harm.

From the back of that painted pony, he had witnessed a thriving populace that completely engulfed the valley below. He could see it again now in minute detail...the river winding among the cottonwoods, the small herds of Indian ponies scattered about lazily grazing on the lush greenery, the smoke curling up from a hundred campfires, the teepees, the children running here and there, intent on their respective games. It was all there, burned into his memory past.

Then he remembered how four years ago, almost to the day, he and Cat had stopped in this very spot, and sitting here in a new Studebaker carriage, he had rediscovered this enchanted place. A few weeks later, he had purchased the land where he had grown to be a man. He and Frank Dodd had branded the first several hundred head of livestock with the T-P branding iron that had been roughly fashioned from discarded scrap metal and a makeshift bellows in a simple homestead blacksmith shop.

Tall realized he had been sitting here for quiet a spell, but he continued to allow himself the luxury to enjoy this moment. He had come to realize that once an experience was claimed by the ravenous jaws of time past it could never be reclaimed. Oh, you might come close, as he was at this very moment, by re-living it in your memory, but it wasn't the same as being there.

The gray in his hair and the gnawing pain in his joints were constant reminders that the day was approaching when his only pleasure would be to sit and indulge himself in reminiscence. That realization only served to make life sweeter. He valued every day and accepted every minute of every day as a generous gift from his Maker above.

His thoughts wandered back to his and Cat's first visit here together. The path they had traveled by buggy back then had been strewn with rocks and limbs and cut across with washes from mountain rainstorms and snowmelt. Tall remembered how he had speculated that it would be many years before Studebaker's horseless carriages would be able to travel this country.

Well, it was not the first time he had miscalculated the genius of modern man. That rugged path had since been claimed by state maintenance crews who had smoothed the road with horse drawn graders and installed tin culverts and timbered bridges, where needed. The road continued westward along the ridge where he and Cat sat in the motorcar.

Eventually it joined into the main northern route that stretched all the way across the country from east to west coasts. Tall reflected how his son, Jesse, had predicted such things just a few years before and had advised him to invest at least a portion of his holdings in the petroleum industry.

Only after Jesse and his son-in-law, John Christopher, had led the way did he do so, but the future in their investments looked brighter every day. There had been some talk of attempting to drill for oil in parts of Wyoming. Although it was known to be somewhat deeper here than in most other places, the payload was expected to be worth the time and effort, especially with new drilling techniques constantly changing and improving.

Change...so much change, Tall thought. He figured there had been about as much change in the four years since he and Cat had sat here in that buggy as there was between then and his first arrival here on that Indian pony. What kind of change did the world hold for his new grandson? After all, he was the reason for this journey. Tall and Cat had received word only a few days ago that Richard Tall Branch had arrived and that he and the new mother were in good health and fine spirits.

When Alaina Marie and John Christopher were married, Tall would not have even allowed himself to hope that they might one day settle in America, let alone in the West. After spending the first two years of marriage traveling Europe and Asia together, they suddenly discovered something missing in their relationship, the bliss of a child to love and to love them back. And the most wholesome environment that either of them could imagine for rearing a child was the wide-open expanse of the wild, wonderful, American West. Thus, John Christopher had followed Tall's example in pleasing a new bride.

He had secretly constructed a beautiful colonial-style mansion near the location of the original homestead cabin to serve as headquarters for the Tee-Pee Land and Cattle Company. Alaina Marie loved it from the start and had immediately taken to Indian Valley Ranch as home sweet home.

John Christopher had not only set out to improve the quality of the cattle herd and establish an equitable cattle market in the area but had applied for and acquired American citizenship…even to the extent of an American spelling of his surname Branch.

Tall chuckled under his breath at the thought. His grandson would be a full-fledged American. That was a pleasing thought.

Tall turned his glance across the motor car to his lifelong best friend and partner in life to find her looking straight into his soul with a knowing smile on her lips. Yes, she had read his thoughts completely from the moment the automobile came to rest fifteen minutes ago. Tall reached for her hand and held it for a long moment as he smiled back. Then he released the hand brake, allowing the motor car to roll down the incline toward the valley below.

THE END

ABOUT THE AUTHOR

John Henry Branch was born and reared among the cotton farms of West Texas. Early in his childhood, he became a "cowboy" at heart with a deep love for horses. With older brothers working on cattle ranches and Roy and Gene cleaning up the west on TV, he found himself longing to follow in their footsteps. He soon realized, of course, that those were the dreams of every young boy and that life had a deeper calling for him. After a four-year tour in the Army, with one year served in Viet Nam, he attended Criswell Bible College in Dallas, Texas, and earned a BA degree in Bible. Upon graduation in 1979, he answered the call of pioneer missions and moved his family to Casper, Wyoming, to pastor a fledgling church there. He would spend several years in the Rocky Mountains of Wyoming and Colorado, working odd jobs to support a wife and three children while pastoring small congregations that were unable to support a full-time pastor. He grew to love the West with all of its colorful history and had a desire to one day share what he saw in that history in the form of a story. That story grew to fruition in the form of CONCHO. It was so well received by family and friends, it wasn't in his heart to say goodbye to Tall and Cat. The gut determination in Tall to make something worthwhile out of the wilderness of Wyoming, and the fire and spit of his wife, Cat, forged a bond that nothing could break. Their children were cut from the same cloth. A wild adventure awaits their young daughter, ALAINA MARIE.